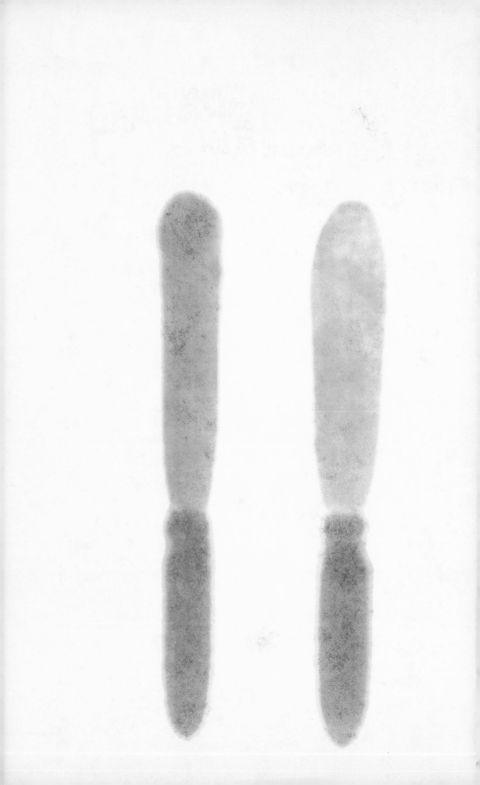

ACES & EIGHTS

ACES & EIGHTS

LOREN D. ESTLEMAN

DOUBLEDAY & COMPANY, INC.
GARDEN CITY, NEW YORK
1981

All of the characters in this book
are fictitious, and any resemblance to actual persons, living or dead, with the
exception of historical personages, is purely coincidental.

Library of Congress Cataloging in Publication Data

Estleman, Loren D.
Aces & eights.

I. Title.
PS3555.S84A64   813'.54
ISBN: 0-385-17469-1
Library of Congress Catalog Card Number 80-2447

To a friend named Huckleberry

Those who see thee in thy full blown pride,
Know little of affections crushed within
And wrongs which frenzy thee.

—Taulford

ACES & EIGHTS

PROLOGUE

SALOON NO. 10

His name is James Butler Hickok, but he has been called Wild Bill for so many years that he no longer answers to anything else. Six foot two in his custom-made boots, he wears a thigh-length Prince Albert coat that accentuates his broad shoulders and narrow waist, black broadcloth trousers, a low-crowned black hat with a sweeping brim, and his most famous possessions, twin Navy Colts riding inside a red sash about his middle with their ivory handles turned forward and the loading gates left open to prevent their sliding out the bottom. His face, seamed now and growing flaccid about the jowls, is handsome in a rough masculine way, receding of chin and hooked of nose, dominated by restless gray eyes and set off by drooping moustaches and blond hair brushed behind his ears and tumbling in ringlets to his shoulders. The face is more famous than President Ulysses S. Grant's, for it has been reproduced in rotogravure in every civilized country on earth. Certainly, as he enters the Deadwood saloon known as No. 10, approaching with feline grace the center table where four men are seated playing draw poker, there is not a customer in the room who doesn't recognize him. He is thirty-nine years old, and he has approximately forty-five minutes to live.

At the table, which is universally regarded as Hickok's headquarters since he and his friends appointed themselves peace officers of this canvas-and-clapboard town of prospectors, gamblers and prostitutes, are Carl Mann, part owner of the saloon, Charles Rich, Con Stapleton, and Captain William Rodney Massey, a Missouri steamboat pilot. After passing time with bartender Harry Young, the newcomer greets the others and, laying aside the sawed-off shotgun he has recently taken to carrying, accepts the only vacant chair, which stands facing the bar with its back to the rear entrance.

"How about changing places, Charley?" he asks Rich in his mild baritone. "I always like to watch who comes in."

Rich, in the act of drawing two cards, grins around his crooked stogie. "You're getting superstitious in your old age," he suggests good-naturedly. "Just like a crib girl."

Hickok colors, but retains his seat. Fortunately for the other player he is in a charitable mood. He once killed a man for calling him Duck Bill in reference to his protruding upper lip.

A professional gambler with whom law enforcement is merely a diversion, the unofficial marshal concentrates on his game, ignoring the conversation that continues in fits and starts between plays. It centers around George Armstrong Custer, who was killed along with his entire command at the Little Big Horn six weeks ago in Montana. Asked for his opinion of the disaster, he makes no reply, instead requesting one card from dealer Carl Mann. Custer and Hickok had been quite close during the latter's scouting days, but that ended when Wild Bill locked up Custer's brother Tom in Hays City on a charge of drunk and disorderly and dealt with two soldiers the offender sent later to retaliate, shooting one and stabbing the other.

The afternoon trade at No. 10 is steady, and no one—including Hickok, determined to break an early losing run—pays much attention to the arrival shortly after 3:00 P.M. of a big man in shabby dress, whose whiskey-flushed face and small, sandy moustaches, together with a broken nose and one crossed eye, make him appear far older than his twenty-seven years. Wild Bill, who is accustomed to attracting admirers, either doesn't notice or ignores the presence of a man from whom he won a substantial sum in yesterday's game. It would not mean much to him in any case, as Jack "Buffalo Curly" McCall is a familiar figure locally, a moocher of drinks and lunches who justifies his existence by swamping out this very saloon part-time.

Casually at first, but with increasing deliberation, the newcomer works his way toward the back door. A few feet short of it he stops and turns, coming up behind Hickok. For some minutes he remains motionless as though watching the game. Suddenly his right hand, which has been inside his coat pocket all this time, is exposed wrapped around the butt of a .45 caliber revolver, the muzzle within three feet of Hickok's head.

Wild Bill and Captain Massey are arguing mildly over the former's habit of sneaking looks at his opponents' discards, referred to as "deadwood." It is a running dispute. The others study their hands in stoic silence, awaiting the expected truce. No one sees the gun.

Later accounts will maintain that in the moment before discharge, McCall cried, "Take that, damn you!" But he is not that stupid and his victim is not that slow to react. The only warning anyone receives is a deafening crash.

Immediately upon penetration, the bullet, traveling at the rate of 810 feet per second, tears through the left and right cerebral hemispheres at a thirty-degree angle downward and to the right, severing simultaneously the centers of thought, action and sensation, bypassing the cerebellum and exiting through the right cheek. From there, its momentum retarded by the mass through which it has passed and by flattening, it traverses thirty inches of open air, enters Captain Massey's forearm resting upon the table, and lodges in the tangle of ligaments and muscles at his elbow. The damage to Massey's arm is not serious, and he will carry the projectile to the grave.

Time seems to freeze as Wild Bill Hickok sits suspended between worlds, staring at the cards in his hand as if he has been dealt one more ace than there is in the deck. Then the wire is broken and he falls backward, tipping over his chair and crashing to the floor. Proponents of his legend will say that in the instant of death his amazing reflexes took over and he actually jerked one of his revolvers from its holster before collapsing. But Hickok wears no holster and his reflexes are as dead as he is.

Transfixed by his success, McCall hovers over the crumpled form longer than judgment dictates. By this time a crowd has begun to gather. He backs stumbling toward the rear door, brandishing his revolver and muttering, "Come on, you sons of bitches." Spotting gold-dust weigher George M. Shingle rising from the table where he has been turning the yellow metal into checks for gambling, McCall snaps the trigger at him, then at aproned Harry Young, who has abandoned his post behind the bar to block the killer's retreat. There are no reports; the rest of McCall's cartridges are duds. But Young hesitates, and for the time being the killer makes good his escape.

The news spreads like fever throughout Deadwood. In minutes

the saloon and the street in front are jammed with the morbidly curious, which in a frontier town includes everyone ambulatory and within earshot. By nightfall many of the miners not now on the scene will have drifted in from their claims to confirm what they will have been told, and the town will be lit up like Saturday night. By that time the opportunists will be at work, hawking locks of hair said to be Hickok's and leaden bits, each advertised as "the one what done it." Later, men with cameras will come to record the scene of the shooting, and still later, men with ink and foolscap to distort the details. By the time the story reaches back East, Jack McCall will have become the ungrateful wretch who killed Wild Bill after the latter staked him five dollars following yesterday's card loss, the number of the saloon will have changed unaccountably, and a score of gullible journalists will be displaying watch fobs and tie tacks made from various items of Hickokiana to even more gullible audiences.

But for now, No. 10 is knee-deep in reality. Most noticeable is the odor, an evil mixture of the normal barroom smells of beer and coal oil and sawdust and sweat, and of spent black powder and perfume —not the scent commonly associated with strike-town prostitutes but Hickok's own, worked into his curls along with his daily oil, a vanity peculiar to French monarchs and frontier dandies. In death it seems stronger.

The legend, however, has one more strand to weave.

Bartender Young struggles to hold back the crowd while saloon owners Carl Mann and Jerry Lewis lift the corpse onto a pair of tables shoved together for the purpose. As they spread a colorful Indian blanket over it, Mann spots young J. Johnson, one of McCall's fellow swampers, pushing in for a closer look.

"Hey, boy, you want to make a dollar?"

"Yes, sir!" responds the youth, after a quick glance around to make sure he is the one being addressed. "What do you want me to do?"

"There's a broom and a bucket of water behind the bar. Get busy and clean up this mess."

The checks have been removed from the table—the other players are neither rich nor foolish—but aside from the dead man's removal everything else is as it was when the shot was fired. Johnson moves the table to one side and discovers a jumble of cards scattered over the floor. From them he selects five that are more bunched together than the others, forming a hand. The Ace of Clubs, the Ace of Diamonds with a heel mark on it, two black Eights, and the Queen of Hearts soiled with a spot of blood. Recognizing their historic value, he secretes the cards in a pocket and will keep them until the day they are stolen from him at a drinking party. James Butler Hickok has died owing the saloon fifty dollars in checks on a mediocre hand of poker.

BOOK ONE

THE PROSECUTION

If you have to shoot a man, shoot him in the guts near the navel. You may not make a fatal shot, but he will get a shock that will paralyze his brain and arm so much that the fight is all over.

—James Butler Hickok, 1871

CHAPTER 1

"General John Quincy Adams Crandall," read the lean man slouched in the stuffed leather armchair, that day's edition of the Yankton *Daily Press and Dakotaian* spread in sixteen gray columns in front of his face. "What's he general of?"

"No one seems to know. But they tell me he turns all sorts of colors if you fail to address him by that title." The speaker, a tweed-suited Southerner with a pouched face and an unruly shock of red hair shot with gray, blew a cloud from his snuff box and inhaled it, all of it. Not a grain floated to the polished wood floor of the austere office the two shared.

"Didn't we have any privates in that war?"

"Speak for yourself, Bluebelly," grinned the man in tweeds.

The narrow, high-ceilinged room smelled of tobacco and old dry leather, the former from a charred ebony-and-amber pipe clenched between the lean man's teeth as far as the joint, the latter from the cracked and thumb-blurred bindings of fat law books squeezed pitilessly onto shelves covering the wall adjacent to the window. Paperwork had overflowed onto the seats of two rolltop desks, leaving only the armchair, in which the pair took turns sitting. Beyond the arched window, ferries could be seen plying the broad brown flatness of the James River beneath motionless black mushrooms of smoke.

"Listen to this." An inveterate train rider, the man with the newspaper folded it expertly into a compact, easily read rectangle two inches wide. He was in his early forties, but already his wavy, dark brown hair was anchored in white side whiskers to the angles of his jaw. His gold-rimmed reading glasses did nothing to soften the Lincolnesque planes of his features. "'Asked what form McCall's defense would take, General Crandall replied: "It is not my client who is going on trial, but the U. S. Constitution itself, which guarantees the citizen's right not to be tried more than once for the same offense. I shall leave the text of my oration up to the members of the First Continental Congress."' Is he really planning to take that line?"

"I doubt it," said the Southerner. "But you can bet he'll give it a whirl. The General's not one to conserve ammunition. What does it say about us?"

The lean man handed him the newspaper. He unfolded it and read:

> Heading the prosecution will be Julian Scout, that same Captain Scout who so successfully defended those members of the 12th New Hampshire charged with desertion in the face of the enemy at Cold Harbor during the late war. Neither he nor his assistant—one T. S. E. Bartholomew, a private practitioner and highly vocal Confederate sympathizer throughout the unpleasantness—could be reached for comment at press time, but other sources indicate a struggle in the offing, as sympathy for the defendant runs high locally.

"Some hatchet job," observed Scout, grinding his teeth on the pipe stem. "I'm a champion of cowards and you're Johnny Reb. Just how vocal were you 'throughout the unpleasantness,' Tessie?"

"I ran for state representative in Minnesota against an abolitionist." Bartholomew flipped the newspaper into the fireplace. Although there was a November chill in the room, no flames burned in the grate; the chimney did not draw well.

"How far do you think Crandall will get with that double-jeopardy plea?"

"That depends on Judge Blair. He's had plenty of time to digest that stuff we gave him on Deadwood's being an outlaw town. All Crandall's got is the Constitution, and you and I both know how well *that* stands up in a modern court of law."

For weeks, controversy had been raging in the press over the legality of a second trial for the accused murderer of James Butler Hickok. Jack McCall had been tried and acquitted by a miners' court in Deadwood the day after the slaying. After fleeing to Laramie, Wyoming, to escape the wrath of Hickok's friends, he had made the mistake of bragging of his deed while drinking in a saloon and was promptly arrested by a deputy U.S. marshal who had been among his audience. The prosecution maintained that the first trial had taken place in a region where constituted law did not prevail and was thus illegal.

"Crandall must know he doesn't have a leg to stand on," suggested Scout.

"Of course. But it's in his client's interest to delay as long as possible. Count on him dragging out every statute in the book. Then, when Blair's reached the end of his tether, he'll plead either self-defense or justifiable homicide and hope he grabs at it."

"I hope it's self-defense. I've witnesses to prove McCall shot Hickok from behind without warning."

"To which Crandall will respond with as many to prove that it was a wise move. Never lose sight of the fact that the victim was a skilled assassin. We'll be on firmer ground if he opts for justifiable, but even then everything will swing on Hickok's character."

Scout's pipe had gone out. He struck a fresh match. "This looked like such a simple case," he growled, between puffs. "You'd think a corpse with a bullet hole in the back of its head was evidence enough to convict anyone, with or without eyewitnesses. And we're loaded with them."

Bartholomew laughed shortly. "Now you're talking like an eastern lawyer. It's not so simple out here where legends are made."

"I wish you'd reconsider and plead this one. You're twice the orator I am."

"In a Yankee court? With my drawl? I'd do more damage than good. Don't sell yourself short, Julian. This case can make you."

"I'm not so sure I want to be made. I like the view from where I'm sitting."

"You can see a lot farther from the judge's bench." Bartholomew was looking at him. He had small, bright eyes that sometimes took on a wicked glitter, as now.

Scout made no reply. He got the tobacco going and shook out the match. "What about the conspiracy angle?"

In his first trial, McCall had blamed Hickok's killing of his brother for his decision to slay the famed gunman. Although subsequent investigation failed to uphold this claim, the revenge angle (and, some asserted, two hundred ounces of gold dust smuggled into the jury room) had led to the defendant's release. But McCall's aborted attempt to escape from the Yankton jail earlier that month had seriously damaged his case the second time around, and he had elected to turn state's evidence by identifying one John Varnes as the man who had paid him to kill Hickok.

Bartholomew shook his head abruptly, frowning. The expression heightened his resemblance to a bulldog. "You'd just be muddying the waters. Varnes has disappeared without a trace and McCall has changed his mind again. It's the prosecution's job to simplify, not complicate. Leave that to the defense. There'll be time enough to bring up the thirty pieces of silver when McCall repeats that story about Hickok killing his brother with a hoe."

"Do you think he'll testify?"

"Probably not. Under cross-examination he'd fold like a pair of deuces on a fifty-dollar bet. But in case I'm wrong you can hit him with his own statement about the blood money."

Scout sucked on his pipe in silence as though considering his partner's advice. In reality he'd already thought about it, just as he'd anticipated almost everything else the older man had said. Eleven years before, Scout had come out of the war a green young lawyer with a raw brilliance for courtroom tactics that had manifested itself, unpopularly, in the court-martial of five soldiers of the 12th New Hampshire regiment accused of cowardice during the fighting at Cold Harbor, Virginia, in 1864. He had won their acquittal on a technicality at the expense of his reputation, as the five had already been convicted in the pages of every major northern newspaper, and after leaving the service he had found every law-firm door closed to him in four eastern states. Penniless, he was contemplating sneaking out of his Pittsburgh hotel to beat the bill when a telegram came offering him employment with the firm of Bartholomew & Hobbs, Yankton, D. T. The wire had been following him from city to city for six weeks, and included a bank draft large enough to settle his debts and make the journey west with some left over.

Immediately he had become the protégé of Bartholomew, a former Minnesota public defender with a flair for politics, who began by instructing him to forget everything he had learned about due process. His next step was to enroll Scout in a dramatics course, where he was taught the techniques of oratory and, in Bartholomew's own words, "the ancient and honorable art of lying." After that the senior attorney had educated him personally in courtroom histrionics, demonstrating the ways in which a juror's emotions could be played upon so that whatever points the opposition brought up, no matter how solid, were rendered meaningless—a practice referred to as "stirring up dust."

Scout's first client after "graduation" was an illiterate ranch hand accused of hamstringing a neighbor's prize racing stallion. His fee was guaranteed by the man's employer. In the face of daunting evidence, through innuendo and delaying tactics which dragged the trial over four exhausting weeks, the young lawyer managed to obtain a hung jury. A second trial was planned, but nagging doubts raised by the amount of insurance the horse's owner had taken out on his property shortly before the mutilation incident unnerved the plaintiff and the charges were dismissed.

There were other cases, some of which Scout lost, but these were far outweighed by his victories. Two years ago he had been offered the appointment as federal prosecutor and, on Bartholomew's advice, had accepted it. Shortly thereafter his mentor sold out his partnership and joined Scout's unofficial staff, where he was paid from the prosecutor's own pocket. A confirmed bachelor of simple tastes, he was more than able to afford his former teacher's salary, a token amount since "Tessie" lived quite comfortably off his investments.

Of late, however, their instructor-pupil relationship had become little more than a ritual, really a brainstorming session during which they developed strategy under the guise of Bartholomew's tutelage. It was a comfortable, productive arrangement, and though both were aware that Scout had learned everything his friend had to teach, neither would say it aloud for fear of upsetting the fine balance. In addition, there was a conviction far back in Julian Scout's mind that Bartholomew was holding something back, and that if they remained together long enough he would play it like a winning hand, to the profit of both.

"One thing bothers me," said the younger man. "If this General Crandall is so good, what's he doing in the public defender's office? Why isn't he in practice for himself, where the money is?"

Bartholomew smiled over his silver snuff box, a present from a wealthy and grateful client. "One might ask the same thing about you," he replied. "The answer would be the same. The man loves the law, and the most interesting cases seem to involve people who can't afford their own attorney."

"You make him sound dedicated."

"He's that. He's also in railroads and rich as Vanderbilt."

"When do we meet him?"

"Not before eight o'clock Wednesday morning, when we select a jury."

Mention of time moved Scout to consult his watch. He started and rose, heading for the clothes tree beside the door. Upright, he had the advantage of nearly a foot over his partner, which never failed to disconcert him. He found it embarrassing being so much taller than most of the frontier heroes that people read about back East.

"Going somewhere?" Bartholomew asked.

"I'm having dinner with Grace Sargent. I've just time to bathe and dress." He shrugged into his greatcoat and placed his narrow-brimmed hat on his head at a jaunty angle. After ten years he had yet to bow to convention and don western garb.

"You've been seeing her for some time now." The crusty old lawyer was smirking as if about to spring an important bit of evidence. "Do I hear the distant clatter of church bells?"

Scout started through the door, ignoring him. Then he paused. "I just thought of something," he said, turning. "Hickok killed men to make a name for himself. McCall shot him for his reputation. I'm out to hang McCall. What does that make me?"

"Senatorial material," said the other, still smirking.

CHAPTER 2

Grace Sargent lived with her mother, or rather her mother lived with her, in a sixteen-room mansion in the city's fashionable neighborhood, a three-story brick box which always reminded Scout, with its latticed windows, of the Yankton jail. It had been built for her by her late husband, an investor in the Great Northern Pacific Railroad, who had shared it with her for three weeks before he was shot to death by a man whose fortune had been wiped out by railroad manipulators during the Panic of 1873. Gray dusk was sifting over the manicured grounds as the prospector alighted from his cab and took the flag path to the front door. The air was raw and held the metallic odor of snow.

The colored maid informed him that Mrs. Sargent would be down shortly and ushered him into the parlor to wait. As always, he felt a trap open in his stomach when he found Dora Hope standing among the settees, chairs, hassocks, and pedestal tables laden with knickknacks which cluttered the otherwise spacious room.

"Mr. Scout," she said, offering her hand.

He accepted it, his fingers feeling the old work calluses only slightly softened by recent years. She was an attractive woman like her daughter, tall, with dark hair still untouched by gray and pulled back not too severely into a bun at the nape of her neck. The bones of her face were prominent and she had the clean profile and corseted bustiness that were the current standard of beauty, but Scout could never look into her crisp gray eyes without feeling inadequate. He muttered some inanity that required no answer, after which there stretched an embarrassing silence.

Desperately, his eyes fell to the newspaper folded atop the tea table between them. "I see you've been reading today's newspaper," he said lamely.

"Yes, I have."

"May I ask what you think of the case?"

"Case?"

Damn her, he thought, she's playing games with me. "The McCall trial, of course." He was painfully conscious of sounding like a self-centered ass.

"Oh yes, that. I'm afraid lurid murder accounts don't interest me."

"It's become more than that. Hickok's fame—"

"—is of little account," she finished. "It won't survive the decade. Of what service is a man like that to society?"

"As I was saying, Hickok's fame has skyrocketed because of the circumstances of his death, and the country is of two minds regarding his slayer. The case is something of a *cause célèbre* locally."

"I find it difficult to work up any sympathy for the fate of a paid assassin, or for that of the man who served him his just deserts."

"The details of their lives are of no importance anywhere outside the courtroom," he countered, warming to the subject. "They're part of frontier mythology now, and with the possible exceptions of women and politics, nothing has sparked more barroom brawls."

"You're being indelicate, Mr. Scout. In any case, it's an untidy business that will reflect poorly upon the reputation of everyone connected with it."

It struck him that for a woman who took no interest in the case, Mrs. Hope seemed quite knowledgeable about its details. "You know that I'm representing the people during the trial," he said.

"Yes, I know."

There was another uncomfortable pause. To Scout's relief, Grace Sargent chose that moment to enter the parlor.

She was shorter than her mother, somewhat plumper of build and fairer, with auburn hair that looked red in the sunlight and a fine dusting of freckles across the top of her cheeks, muted but not obliterated beneath an expert application of powder. Her eyes were more blue than gray and she wore a dress of old gold taffeta in marked contrast to Mrs. Hope's drab trappings of no particular hue, beneath the floor-length hem of which flashed an occasional teasing glimpse of black patent-leather toe as the younger woman approached amid rustling petticoats—a sound that never failed to stir her escort. She wore her hair up beneath a crownless hat decked with ostrich plumes and secured at a rakish angle with an invisible pin.

"Bending each other's ear as usual, I see," she said, smiling.

Scout bowed over her proffered hand and commented upon her loveliness. She blushed prettily. Although he had known enough women to recognize this as an act, it always gave him a warm feeling in his chest.

"I hope you haven't been staring at each other all this time," she said.

"We were discussing the man Mr. Scout hopes to hang," replied her mother.

"That again." She made a face. "Mother's spoken of nothing else since that man McCall was captured. She takes six newspapers and reads them all. You'd be wise to make her your assistant, Julian; I'm sure she knows quite as much about the case as you do."

Scout smiled discreetly at Mrs. Hope's discomfort.

"There's nothing else to do out here, except sew," she said, rallying. "And I refuse to sew."

This time his smile was more polite. He found Grace's rapport with her mother refreshing, but there was something about it that rang false, as if the two were craning their necks to see each other around something that neither wanted to acknowledge. He was glad when he and Grace took their leave.

"Mother took in sewing to support us after Father died," explained Grace, when they were in his cab rattling over the frozen street surface. She was huddled in a heavy wrap a shade darker than her dress. "She doesn't like to be reminded of it."

"She doesn't care much for me." He charged his pipe and lit it. Grace liked the smell of tobacco, another reason he enjoyed her company.

"You mustn't take it personally, Julian. It's this country she resents, not you. She's afraid you'll marry me and we'll be stuck out here forever."

He glanced at her, startled. But she was watching the scenery roll past in the light of the street lamps, her cheeks flushed from the cold. For a moment he had thought she'd guessed his reason for asking her out tonight. "I don't know what she's got to be afraid of," he said then. "You've spent most of your life out here."

"Not really. I was five when we joined the wagon train bound for Oregon before the war."

"All right, so I'm a liar for five years."

"More like twelve. Pneumonia killed Father when I was eight, after we had settled in Kansas. Mother sold the farm and we moved to a rooming house in Kansas City until she had enough money to send me back East to finish my schooling. No one was happier than she when I married Edgar because she was sure that we would all be living in Providence. Then Edgar decided to move out here so he could be near his investment."

"That must have made him popular." He wished he could think of something to say that would change the subject. Her late husband was not one of his favorite topics.

"Let's say she was not amused," she replied, smiling. "He built the house mainly to please her, not that it did any good. She's cursed him for it ever since he was—ever since the incident because it's too expensive to sell, and she's got too much Scottish blood in her to go home and keep on paying servants to care for a house no one is living in, no matter how much Edgar left us. So she goes on hoping that a buyer will appear before 'some western bumpkin,' as she puts it, claims my hand." She patted his arm. "You're the culmination of her worst fears."

For a moment his heart soared, but then he realized she was only teasing. Somewhat testily, he said, "Why hasn't she sent you back alone?"

"Because I'm thirty years old, and no longer do everything my mother tells me."

He wanted to pursue the subject, but the cab had reined up before the restaurant and there was a spattering of people on the boardwalk within earshot. He climbed out, helped her down, and paid the driver.

The restaurant was new, established with Yankton's burgeoning carriage trade in mind. Rough language was not permitted, brass cuspidors were numerous and placed discreetly, and each table sported its own red-and-white-checked cloth and centerpiece of artificial flowers. To preserve the genteel atmosphere, a bouncer whose fine tailored suit did little to disguise his resemblance to a bull buffalo stood in the shadows at the back of the room beyond reach of the hanging Rochester lamps, scanning the clientele for trouble-makers. His attention kept returning to a couple seated near the kitchen door, the male half of which, thickset and strangling in a yellowing celluloid collar and wilted necktie, was conversing in a loud, drunken voice with his mousy blond companion over a forgotten meal. She ignored him, intent on chasing a stationary brussels sprout around her plate with a swaying fork.

Scout, a veteran of New York dining establishments that were long on atmosphere and short on edibles, played it safe and ordered roast beef for himself and Grace, with the house wine. He wanted nothing to spoil this evening. The beef turned out to be surprisingly tender if not particularly tasty, a condition which he suspected represented hours of pounding with a cleaver in this land of stringy longhorns. The wine was no more than adequate, but then he hadn't expected much. When they had finished eating:

"Julian, is it very dangerous?"

"I'm sure it isn't or they wouldn't serve it."

"I don't mean the meal, silly." She shook her fist at him in mock anger. "I mean the trial. I've been hearing rumors—"

"—about McCall's gang threatening to shoot up the courtroom? I've heard them too. Forget them. What kind of gang does a man need to swamp out a saloon?"

"Not those. You know that there are a lot of men around the territory who were glad to learn of Hickok's death. They don't like the idea of his killer having to stand trial."

He touched his lips with his napkin. "You've been reading your mother's newspapers. I don't doubt that there are some demented souls out there who regard McCall as a hero, but they're like him, cowardly. That kind is content just to harangue others over a cheap beer."

"McCall wasn't."

"You're beginning to sound like the heroine of a dime novel," he said, grinning. "I'm not going out to fight a duel."

She looked embarrassed. "All the same, I wish you hadn't let your partner talk you into accepting the case."

"What made you think he talked me into it?"

"Don't pretend with me, Julian. You know how he's always pushing you. He never made it in politics, so he's doing the next best thing. He wants to point to you someday and boast how he manufactured a congressman."

He remembered Bartholomew's comment about his being senatorial material and grew angry. "Tessie's a fine attorney who had the misfortune to be born a Southerner at a time when it was passing out of fashion. I'm his partner, not his puppet."

She sipped her wine and said nothing. His anger turned inward; he hadn't wanted the evening to go in this direction. He was grateful when the waiter returned with the check and commented discreetly on his excellent taste in companions. By the time he had departed to wait on another table, she had thawed visibly.

"Someday I'll find out how you arranged that." Her smile was rueful.

"Grace, your husband was an older man, wasn't he?"

"Older than what?" Unruffled by the blurted question, she beamed at him teasingly over her wine. The pale red liquid threw spots of reflected light up into her face.

He shifted uncomfortably in his seat. "What I mean is, did it bother you to be married to a man who was so much more . . . mature . . . than you?"

She watched him in silence, still smiling. He had seen comprehension dawning in her eyes. Her cheeks were flushed again, but not from cold or even embarrassment. It was her second glass of wine. He hurried on before she could answer.

"For an attorney, I'm not expressing myself very well," he said. "What I mean—"

Her fingers touched the back of his hand, stopping him. "I know what you mean." She seemed about to continue when the focus of her eyes shifted suddenly to something beyond his right shoulder. He turned his head to see a man approaching on unsteady legs.

It was the drunk he had observed earlier talking to the blonde. He was a big man, too big for the suit he was wearing, the sleeves of which fell several inches short of the ends of his wrists and which was badly in need of brushing. He had undone his collar finally. His face was a beefy slab with brutal, half-finished features tanned as far as his forehead, where a pale band betrayed a crown unaccustomed to being naked. He was extremely bowlegged and wore high-topped boots with two-inch heels. Beyond his bulk, the prosecutor could see that the blonde had abandoned her pursuit of the brussels sprout and was sitting with her chin cupped in her hand staring into space.

"You'd be Julian Scout." The brute pronounced the name slowly, spitting out the last half as if it were a dead fly in a mouthful of butter.

"Have we been introduced?" Scout started to rise. A hand like a coal shovel descended to his shoulder, holding him down.

"Don't get up. This ain't going to take long. I seen your pitcher in the Laramie paper. That artist fellow got you down real good. You're the bastard wants to stretch Buffalo Curly's neck."

"There's a lady present," the other reminded him angrily. He felt foolish saying it without getting up, but there was no arguing with the weight on his shoulder. He was aware that cutlery had ceased clanking around him and that every eye in the room was on them.

"I was in Abilene the time Hard-ass Hickok gunned down Phil Coe in cold blood. Any bastard that killed that back-shootin' son of a bitch Hickok is my friend."

The drunk swayed backward on his heels momentarily. It was the opportunity for which Scout had been waiting. He shoved away the man's arm with the heel of a hand and pushed to his feet. Annoyed to find his napkin still clutched in one hand, he threw it down onto the table. By this time the drunk, evidently convinced that he had been assaulted, charged forward, cocking back a huge left fist. Scout moved to block it.

They never made contact. Just as the blow was hurled, the bouncer, materializing suddenly from the shadows, caught it from behind. The drunk's forward momentum would have pitched him over onto his face were it not for the man holding his wrist. He had an inch on his captor and nearly fifty pounds, but his bulk was mostly fat while the restaurant employee's was solid meat. The bouncer jerked the drunk's arm downward and up behind his back, twisting it. Frantically, his prisoner swept aside the skirt of his coat and reached for something that shone dully inside the waistband of his pants.

"Watch it, he's got a pistol!" barked Scout. Grace screamed.

There was a deafening explosion. Scout caught his breath, in his confusion certain that he had been shot. But the drunk was standing there blinking stupidly, the muzzle of his big revolver pointing at the floor. It wasn't smoking.

The prosecutor half-turned to see United States Marshal Burdick standing thirty paces away, sideways, his long right arm extended at shoulder level, a big Navy Colt growing out of his hand and pointing at the drunk. A big man except when compared with such as the drunk and the bouncer, he still had his checked napkin thrust inside his high starched collar. His meal lay half-finished in a dish on the table beside which he stood. Black-powder smoke swirled about him and a thin stream of plaster was leaking from a hole in the ornate tin ceiling above his head. In a single, fluid motion he had drawn the revolver from beneath his coat, fired a shot in the air, and pulled down on the drunk while the latter was still bringing his own cumbersome weapon into play.

"Killing spoils my appetite," he told the drunk calmly. "I'd be obliged if you'd hand that big Walker to Gedaliah there and then mount up and start riding. You can spit chew over the border from here."

The man with the Walker Colt hesitated briefly, but Scout suspected this had more to do with sluggish reflexes than with defiance, for the six-shooter remained rock-steady in the marshal's hand. Gedaliah, the bouncer, closed his fingers over the gun and it was relinquished readily. Only then did he release his grip on the drunk's arm. The headwaiter, a fat Frenchman whose chins spilled over his boiled collar like too much dough in a small pan, brought him his hat. Glowering, he jammed the sweat-stained Stetson onto his head and set a tack for the front door, scarcely glancing at the table where he had left his stupefied companion, since deserted.

Scout, thanking the marshal, was the first to break the silence. Burdick waved it away with the barrel of his gun.

"I guess you lawyer fellows don't get much practice with drunks outside the courtroom," he said, returning the revolver to his left holster, butt forward.

The prosecutor ground his teeth at that. Despite the headwaiter's protests that the meal was on the house, he paid for it and collected his coat and hat and Grace's wrap. "Let's go," he said stiffly, holding the last garment for her.

"Would you like to finish the conversation elsewhere?" she asked on the way out. Many pairs of eyes followed them.

"Some other time."

CHAPTER 3

Patrons of a popular Yankton dining establishment were witnesses to a violent and drunken altercation between Julian Scout, the people's representative in the forthcoming murder trial of Jack McCall, and an anonymous customer Monday night. Although details are not known at this time, observers relate that the scuffle erupted over a woman, and that United States Marshal Burdick was forced to separate the combatants. Both parties were then obliged to quit the premises.

Scout found the *Daily Press and Dakotaian* open and folded to the one-inch item in the lead column on page one, on the table reserved for the prosecution when he arrived at the Federal Court building Wednesday morning. Bartholomew, seated at the table in his best gray three-piece suit, kept his eyes on the empty judge's bench while his partner read. They were alone in the oak-paneled room.

"Sons of bitches," breathed the other, pushing the paper away. "They've made it sound like I was drunk too."

"Had you been drinking?" The older attorney had drawn his snuff box from a pocket and was fingering it longingly. But some judges objected to the habit, and he preferred not to antagonize the bench this early in the proceedings.

"Two glasses of wine, Tessie! With a full meal! I told you all about it yesterday. Don't tell me you believe these—these—" He snapped his hand at the folded newspaper.

"Calumnies," Bartholomew finished. "I believe you, but I don't count. The dozen men we choose today to hear our case, they're the ones that count. How will we challenge them on it? Ask them if they read that piece about the people's attorney brawling in public and if it would affect their decision? Damn it, Julian, I thought I'd taught you the importance of maintaining a low profile when you're preparing a case."

"What am I supposed to do, crawl into a hole until the jury reaches a verdict?"

The last part of Scout's question was whispered. The bailiff had entered through the main doors at the head of a line of men in clothes of varying quality and was directing them to the spectator pews behind the attorneys. This was the group from which twelve would be selected to determine the trial's outcome. Their shuffling footsteps echoed sibilantly in the rafters.

"Who do you suspect planted the story?" Bartholomew murmured.

"How should I know? It could have been anyone." Scout drew his briefs from a scuffed leather case and began shuffling them industriously but with no apparent aim. "Newspapers these days have stringers everywhere."

"I don't think it was one of their regular stringers."

Scout looked at him. "You're talking like a lawyer. What are you trying to say?"

"You know as well as I do that just as many cases are won outside the courtroom as inside. What do you think?"

"You suspect Crandall?"

"Don't look so incredulous." He poked the snuff box into a vest pocket. "It wouldn't be the first time a defense attorney tried for a change of venue by claiming press prejudice. Usually, though, they plant something that they can claim damages their own case. If this is his work, you've got to hand it to the General for originality."

"If he did plant it, he'll be counting on us to lodge the complaint."

"The best confidence men let the mark make the offer."

"In which case we don't oblige him."

Bartholomew shrugged. "We'll stand the risk of pleading a prejudiced case. McCall won't be tried a third time if we fail here. You see how he's hemmed us in."

"Are you advising me to move for a delay?"

"You'd be playing right into Crandall's hands if you did."

"Damn it, Tessie, as a partner you're frustrating as hell." Scout glowered at the papers in his hands. "No delays. It's this one or nothing."

The other didn't appear to be listening. His gaze was directed toward the side door, where the court clerk, a tiny, balding man with fluffy white side whiskers, black folder in hand, was deep in conversation with a stout man scarcely taller, whose florid complexion and thick crop of soft gray hair evoked memories of Mr. Pickwick. Behind them, resignedly awaiting his turn at the doorway, towered a third party fully ten inches their superior. He was gaunt and hollow-cheeked and wore his black hair plastered to his skull on either side of a part the width of a pencil. Black-rimmed pince-nez straddled his fleshless nose, attached by a ribbon to the lapel of his swallowtail coat. His color was gray in contrast to the heavier man's high flush.

"Of course, we can't be sure that the General is the one responsible for the story," remarked Bartholomew. "Why don't you ask him?" He inclined his head toward Mr. Pickwick.

As if aware of the attention he was getting, the plump man broke off his discussion and came over to the prosecution table, moving gracefully in spite of his ungainly build. He wore a soft brown suit with a watch chain strung across the vest and a gold-mounted elk's tooth for a fob. His face was round and he was smiling. It was a bright smile, and the teeth thus displayed appeared to be all his. His grip when he shook Scout's hand was firm as expected. The prosecutor didn't trust men with firm handshakes.

"An honor, counselor." Crandall's voice was deep and sonorous, his tones those of a trained orator. "Your defense of the 12th New Hampshire was a triumph of justice over barbarism."

"Your reputation precedes you as well, counselor," Scout murmured.

"General," greeted Bartholomew, with a nod. His hands remained in his pockets.

Crandall studied him quizzically. "Have we met?"

"Not exactly. I've seen you work. I was in the gallery the first day of the Jordan trial." He introduced himself. Crandall nodded.

"Bartholomew, of course. I should have guessed. I read in the *Press and Dakotaian* that you were assisting Scout. That was a sad case, Jordan's. He was given twenty-five years, you know. But I at least saved him from the hangman."

At mention of the Yankton newspaper, Bartholomew and Scout

exchanged quick glances. But nothing in the defense attorney's voice or manner indicated that he had had any personal dealings with the organ. While he was speaking, the gray-complexioned man with the pince-nez joined them. Crandall placed a paternal hand on his arm.

"Orville Gannon, gentlemen," he announced. "He'll be assisting me on this one."

The newcomer regarded them each in turn with a cold blue eye. He made no effort to shake hands, which suited the prosecutor. Still, he studied Gannon with interest, for he had sensed a stiffening on Bartholomew's part at the mention of the name. He saw nothing disturbing. If anything, the silent man seemed completely lacking in personality.

"Orville Gannon," echoed Bartholomew thoughtfully. "This case fairly rings with familiar names."

For a brief moment Crandall's oily manner faltered. His brows rose. "I hadn't realized you knew each other."

"We've never met."

The General's mouth pursed on the verge of a question.

"Mr. Bartholomew and I opposed each other on an assault case some years ago." Gannon's voice was as cold as he seemed, with all the inflection of a humming rail. His eyes, magnified by the thick spectacles, were on Scout's partner. "I was engaged by the plaintiff to head the prosecution, but I didn't appear in court. Another attorney pleaded the case."

"And now you've switched roles." The senior defense counsel had regained his bluster. "What a strange profession we practice."

There the conversation ended, and after a few moments during which all parties seemed to be casting about for something else to say—except Gannon, who remained evidently untouched by anything approaching emotion—McCall's lawyers repaired to the defense table amid patently insincere tidings of good fortune.

"We certainly learned a lot from that confrontation," Scout muttered, taking his seat beside his partner.

"What did you expect? Good actors make great lawyers." He paused and seemed about to add something but for the interruption of the clerk, who announced Judge Blair.

The magistrate was taller than Scout, nearly as tall as Gannon, and even thinner. Far from concealing it, his voluminous black robes accentuated his gauntness, hanging in folds from his high narrow

shoulders and rustling as he strode to the bench. His hair was fine
and white and the bones of his face seemed to show through his taut
flesh, which was blue almost to the point of translucence. His eyes
were dark hollows beneath the bushy white overhang of his brows.
He was clean-shaven, despite the fact that the thought of a razor
scraping that fragile skin made Scout cringe.

After seating himself and cracking his waiting gavel to signal everyone else to do the same, Blair employed a mild witticism to put
the potential jurors at their ease. Without waiting to see if it had
worked, he greeted both counsels and requested them to proceed
with their selection. His voice, though shallow in the face of advancing age, held a surprising resonance that carried to every corner.

The rest of the morning was spent scrutinizing the candidates,
who were called one by one to the jury box to answer questions
about themselves. Crandall, who was permitted more challenges in
defense of his client, used them sparingly but with an expert hand,
ruthlessly weeding out the undesirables. Scout challenged but once,
when a candidate expressed the belief that no man accused of killing
an ex-Union soldier could expect justice from a Yankee court. He
had been about to disqualify another when Bartholomew stopped
him.

"Stand pat," whispered his partner. "Make him think you're playing an unbeatable hand."

"Seems like one hell of a risk," Scout growled.

"That's why it's called gambling."

The jury as selected consisted of John Treadway, Hiram A. Dun-
ham, William Box, George Pike, Lewis Clark, West Negus, Charles
Edwards, Isaac N. Esmay, Henry T. Mowry, Nelson Armstrong,
James A. Withee, and Martin L. Winchell. When they had been
dismissed and the judge was gathering his notes, Crandall and Gannon nodded to the prosecution team and departed through the main
doors. The latter remained at their table after Blair had left, Scout
putting away his briefs, Bartholomew, safe now, employing his
snuff.

"What's the story on this Orville Gannon?" asked the prosecutor.
He had secured his briefcase and was scraping the bowl of his pipe
with a pen knife.

His partner sneezed into a handkerchief. "He's about your age,
single, the end of a long line of attorneys in a family that goes back

to Plymouth Rock. He practiced in Connecticut for a while, then came west in sixty-seven after the first strikes were made at the Sweetwater River in Wyoming to render his services to wronged miners. Since then he's branched out. That's as much as I know, except for the fact that he's brilliant."

"Is he as good as Crandall?"

"He's better, but in a different area. He's no orator. I doubt that he's ever pleaded a case in court, or if he has it was only to confirm his suspicions that he was more effective working beyond the limelight. That brain of his is crammed with every statute and precedent drafted since the Constitution. When it comes to preparing a case for trial he has no master."

Scout paused in the midst of lighting his pipe. "He worries you, doesn't he? I saw how you reacted when Crandall introduced him."

"Why not?" said the other. "He beat the pants off me in that assault case."

The air in the rickety coach was murky with cigar smoke and lamp haze and night. In the inadequate light, the four men seated facing each other across a battered steamer trunk were forced to hold their cards two inches in front of their faces to read them. Two hours before, the faces' owners had been strangers; soon they would be again. The game was the only thing they had in common.

Most of the money on the trunk was gathered in a disheveled heap in front of the drummer, a youngish man with a derby, a natty moustache, and a round, glistening face flushed with victory and the influence of a steel hip flask. When he raised the pot, the man at his left, a heavy-faced Indian whose scarred right cheek twitched with every other heartbeat, cursed in Spanish and threw down his cards. That left the drummer, a stout, gray-bearded land speculator from Pennsylvania, and the man called Smith. But for them the car was deserted.

"Let's see your cards," drawled the last. He had a faint southern accent.

The drummer squinted at him. Sitting upright across from him, Smith was clearly visible from the neck down, where the lamp's greasy yellow glow fell across a well-cut suit wrinkled from being rolled up and carried behind the cantle of a saddle, and long hands with narrow fingers. From there up, only the highlights of a slim face were discernible.

"Let's see your money," the drummer replied. "Mr. Smith." He employed the name as if it were a dubious title.

There was a brief silence, and then one of Smith's hands disappeared. The drummer stiffened and reached for the bulldog pistol he carried behind his belt in the small of his back. When the hand returned with a fistful of bills he relaxed.

"Full house, queens high." The drummer spread his cards on the trunk.

"That takes care of me," sighed the speculator, folding his hand. Smith tossed down his own without a word.

The drummer was raking the pot into his upended derby, revealing a head of scanty copper-colored hair, when the conductor leaned in through the door connecting the cars.

"Sioux City, gents."

"Just in time," grinned the winner, rising. Cradling the hat lovingly, he pulled down his heavy sample case from the overhead rack, nodded to the others, and started down the aisle, weaving a little more than the car's rocking demanded.

"That's my money you're leaving with," Smith said quietly.

"No, it's mine," tossed the other, over his shoulder.

The shot crashed in the confined space. The drummer cried out, dropping his hat and sample case and clawing for the support of a nearby seat. Once he had it, he grabbed his foot and stared back uncomprehendingly at the revolver in Smith's hand. Smoke whirled about the car's interior.

"You shot my foot!" he cried.

"Just your bootheel." Smith's voice was even as always. "Come back here and play cards."

"My stop's coming up!" The drummer was busy examining the sole of his shoe, which was indeed heelless.

"It's coming quicker than you think if you don't pick up that money and get back here by the time I count ten."

The connecting door flew open and the conductor rushed in, a Remington revolver in hand. He found the four men seated as he had left them. "What the hell's going on? What was that shot?"

"I heard it too," drawled Smith from the shadows. "It came from outside."

The conductor peered at him but was unable to make out his features. "Then how come I smell gunpowder?"

"I don't know. Does anyone else smell gunpowder?" He looked from one uneasy face to another, finishing with the drummer's, which was pasty white. "No one smells gunpowder. I guess it's your imagination."

There was something in his tone that made the railroader think of his wife and the eight years that still separated him from his pension, and he lowered the revolver.

"I guess maybe it was," he mumbled, and turned away.

"When do we reach Yankton?" Smith asked him.

"Two hours," said the other. "Maybe you got business there."

"Maybe I do. In any case it's hardly your affair, is it? Five-card draw, gentlemen—nothing wild." Slim hands shuffled the deck.

CHAPTER 4

He was a big man, much of that bigness concentrated around his middle, though he could not quite be called fat, just beefy. His brow was low and retreating, sandy hair darkened with pomade and combed carefully across his skull in a partially successful attempt to straighten the curls, neck pink and naked-looking where a barber hired by General Crandall had trimmed the nape. His moustache had been trimmed as well so that it barely reached the top of his lip in a pencil-thin line straight across, but here the scissorswork had been ill-advised since it added to the overall shiftiness of his appearance. A broken nose and one eye turned inward as if to observe what its mate was up to contributed to the untrustworthy image. The suit was new, as was his shirt, starched white cotton with a black check, which crackled when he moved. He had refused to wear a necktie. Crandall and Gannon had conferred at some length over whether to buy him new boots as well, only to agree that his broken-down brown pair would help to create the impression of a man accustomed to honest toil. He had stolen them off a sleeping drunk in a Deadwood livery stable after his old ones had worn through at the soles. Rising from his seat at the defense table, he folded his big, broken-knuckled hands with their heavily shackled wrists in front of him and stood mute as his attorneys had counseled him when asked by the old man behind the bench how he pleaded.

"Enter that as a plea of not guilty," Blair instructed the court recorder, a young man seated at a tiny desk to the right of the bench. McCall sat, flanked by counsel, his chains clanking. Crandall was on his feet again an instant later.

"Your Honor, defense moves for a dismissal on the grounds that the incident under examination took place in a lawless region entirely outside the jurisdiction of this court."

There was an audible sigh among the spectators, as of the sudden release of tension following the opening shot on a field of battle. The pews were packed, and the crowd left standing at the back of the room was larger than the entire assembly on most normal days. Several of the bonneted ladies held covered picnic baskets on their laps; the odor of pickles was at war with the older, more established smells of varnish and furniture oil and the oppressive stench of steaming wool. A heavy, wet snow was falling outside, and soaked overcoats and mufflers were drying slowly in the heat of a potbelly stove in the corner next to the judge's chambers. A number of men in ill-fitting suits shared the front row, pencils poised over ruled pads. Upon entering and seeing them, Scout had wondered if any of them was the one who had written up the confrontation in the restaurant.

At the General's motion, Bartholomew, seated beside Scout at the prosecution table, turned to his partner with a wry grin and an almost imperceptible shake of his head. It seemed to say, "The bastard's coming out swinging."

The prosecutor was less philosophic. In one fell swoop his opponent had destroyed the state's basis for trying McCall a second time, by turning the charge that the location of the first trial was an outlaw town to his own advantage. Now Scout would be forced to fall back on the shakier alternative he and Bartholomew had discussed before.

Judge Blair, who had donned a pair of wire-rimmed eyeglasses to peruse the sheaf of papers placed before him by the clerk, frowned and shifted his gaze to Crandall.

"Overruled, General," he said. "The Black Hills entered federal jurisdiction the day Congress opened the region to prospectors."

Crandall, still standing, hands in pockets, was unruffled. "In that case, Your Honor, defense moves for dismissal on the grounds that no man may be tried twice for the same offense, Mr. McCall having been acquitted by a legal jury in a legal town on August third of this year."

Blair had a hand in front of his mouth, all too obviously concealing a smile. Then he became stern. "Your point is well taken, General, though your verbiage could stand improvement. Outside the bailiwick of Judge Isaac Parker, which is atypical, every man convicted in an American court of law is entitled to request a second trial. Once acquitted, however, he cannot be forced to defend himself again."

"Is the bench instructing the jury at this time?" the General asked smoothly. "If it is, I must register an objection."

"Overruled."

"Exception, Your Honor."

"Noted." Blair's eyes flicked to the prosecutor. "Mr. Scout?"

Scout rose and rested his fingertips on the tabletop. "Your Honor, it is the state's contention that the miner's court which acquitted Jack McCall, *alias* Bill Sutherland"—he relished the effect of ringing in the pseudonym sometimes employed by the defendant—"was an illegal body, convened in a music hall hardly in keeping with the issue's solemnity, and tried by an illegally selected jury under the dubious direction of an unqualified judge chosen by an unruly mob, and that therefore the verdict was unlawful."

Crandall rebutted without waiting for the judge's invitation. "The defense submits that Judge W. Y. Kuykendall was and is a duly appointed magistrate conforming to the laws of Dakota Territory and the United States, elected by a democratic majority to swear in a proper jury and to oversee a speedy and public trial as guaranteed by the U. S. Constitution. That body was convened not in a music hall as my esteemed colleague suggests, but in a respectable theater, which was the only place suitable, a courthouse not yet having been erected, and which was more than adequate for the purpose. Your Honor has read the transcripts from that trial and should be aware—"

"Objection!" Scout, who had sat down, leaped to his feet. "No such transcripts have been introduced into evidence."

"Sustained!" Blair rapped his gavel. For the first time there was color in his cheeks. "Gentlemen, be seated. Bailiff, remove the jury."

The uniformed officer, a thickset man of middle age with a magnificent blond handlebar moustache, ushered the jurors out through the side door. Blair removed his glasses and sat back in silence until it was closed. Then, gravely:

"General, you have practiced long enough to be aware of the procedure by which evidence is introduced in a modern court of law. In addition, you know full well that the 'transcripts' of which you spoke are not that at all, but merely accounts of the trial as it was reported in the Deadwood newspaper. I don't know if you were attempting to prejudice the jury or merely testing me, nor do I care. But if you repeat this practice I shall find you in contempt of court and direct the bailiff to remove you to the city jail." He turned to the officer. "Summon the jurors."

Scout studied Crandall as the jury filed back into the box, but could see no sign that his opponent was in any way abashed by the judge's admonition. If anything, as he sat whispering with Gannon, he looked as if he had just won an important point. Bartholomew supplied the answer.

"He's got Blair reacting just the way he wants. Removal of either counsel means a recess, something any public defender worth his salt would gladly spend a night or two in jail to get. Meanwhile, his partner is free to develop strategy."

The prosecutor wondered idly how many dank cells had been graced by the General's presence during his years with the bar.

"The jury will disregard defending counsel's reference to transcripts of proceedings not at issue in this court. As for your motion for dismissal, General, I have decided to overrule it on the grounds presented by the state. This trial will proceed."

Scout felt no elation at being upheld. He thought the judge guilty of a blunder in allowing the jury time to mull over Crandall's mention of transcripts before instructing them to disregard it. Now the prosecutor would be fighting the specter of that acquittal throughout the proceedings.

"There being no further motions," said Blair, "I will ask the state to call its first witness."

George M. Shingle, the gold-dust weigher at Saloon No. 10, was a brawny man with big hands and a livid strawberry mark covering the right side of his large face, not a whit obscured by the handlebar moustache he wore with waxed points extending beyond his pendulous ears. His black hair was parted in the middle and slicked down on both sides. As he was being sworn in, his left palm all but obscured the Bible in the bailiff's hand.

"Mr. Shingle," Scout began, after the witness' name and occupation had been established, "did you know the deceased?"

"I should say I did." His voice was deep and gravelly, fitted for rougher garb than the dark brown suit he was wearing with a narrow yellow stripe. "We've been crossing trails since 1866, me and old Wild Bill."

"When you say 'Wild Bill,' you're referring to James Butler Hickok, the murdered man?"

"Objection." Crandall spoke mildly, retaining his seat. "Prosecution has not established that any murder was committed."

"Sustained." The judge glowered at the prosecutor. "My warning to General Crandall applies to you as well, Mr. Scout."

"I'm sorry, Your Honor. I'll rephrase the question. 'Wild Bill' was the name by which you knew the deceased, was it not, Mr. Shingle?"

At a loss as to what to do with his hands, the witness leaned forward finally and let them dangle between his knees. "Well, and I reckon that's what most folks called him. I never heard no one say 'James Butler' when he was around, though he did usually sign himself 'J. B. Hickok.' "

"I see. What did Wild Bill do for a living?"

"When he first come to Deadwood he staked a claim and done some mining, but hard work never did agree with him, so he turned to gambling. Bill was a mighty good poker player. I reckon that if someone was to tote it all up they'd find that he spent more time at the table than just about anywhere else."

"Was that all he did?"

"Oh, hell, no." He smiled nervously, showing a gold crown among surprisingly well-kept teeth. "When I first come to know him he was scouting for the army, and before that I'm told he was a regular war hero fighting Johnny Reb and before that he was a stage hostler at Rock Creek Station in Nebrasky, where he got into a fracas with the McCanles gang but come out of it all of a piece, which is more than I can say for them McCanleses. Since then he done some marshaling here and there, places like Hays City and Abilene—which is where he got his reputation—I don't know what all else. You might say he done a little of everything worth talking about."

"By 'marshaling,' do you mean that he had been an officer of the law?"

"I didn't think it meant nothing else."

Mild laughter rippled through the gallery at Shingle's remark, quickly stilled by a fierce glance from the bench. Scout, who had not moved from behind his table, smiled to show that he had a sense of humor. He let it fade naturally.

"To your knowledge, Mr. Shingle, was Hickok marshaling at the time he was killed?"

"Your Honor, I fail to see where Mr. Scout's questions are leading." The General had a typewritten sheet of paper in front of him and was punching holes in the margins with a pencil.

"Would you mind filling us in, counselor?" the judge asked Scout.

"I hope to demonstrate the enormity of the crime, Your Honor, by establishing that the deceased was a peace officer."

"A peace officer has neither more nor less right to live than any other citizen, counselor. General Crandall's objection, if it is an objection"—he looked to the defender, who assured him that it was—"is sustained."

Scout shrugged acquiescence. He had made his point. "Mr. Shingle, would you tell the court where you were on the afternoon of Wednesday, August 2, 1876?"

"Where I usually am," the witness replied. "At my table in No. 10, weighing out gold dust on my scales."

"What transpired on that day?"

Shingle cleared his throat, a dry, racking noise. Scout filled a glass with water from the pitcher on his table and brought it to him, returning immediately to his place to avoid dividing the jury's attention. Every eye in the room, with the exception of Crandall's, busy aiming his pencil at a fresh sheet of paper, and of Gannon's, directed toward a wide-ruled pad upon which he was scribbling notes, followed the dip and rise of the witness' Adam's apple as he chugged down the contents of the glass. When it was empty he set it down on the rail in front of him with a soggy thump.

"There was a game of five-card draw going on at the center table," he began, mopping his lips with a red handkerchief drawn from his hip pocket. "The players were Cap'n Massey, Charley Rich, Carl Mann—one of my bosses—and Con Stapleton. I reckon it'd been going on for about a half hour when Bill come in carrying his shotgun. He stopped long enough to shoot the breeze with Harry Young, who was tending bar—I didn't hear what they said—and then he come over to join the game. But the only empty chair had the back door behind it, so Bill asked Charley would he change places."

"One moment," Scout interrupted. "Why was it so important that he sit somewhere else?"

"Bill always liked to have a wall behind him, on account of he was scared of getting shot in the back. Charley was sitting against the bar, which for Bill was the best seat at the table."

"I see. Please go on."

"Well, Charley joshed him out of it, claimed he was getting superstitious in his old age. So Bill took the other seat. Oh, and I forgot to say he laid down his shotgun on the next table—that was before he sat down. Carl had me bring Bill some checks to play with, on credit like always. After that things got pretty quiet, until Jack McCall showed up."

"Did you recognize him?"

"Only by sight. He played poker with Bill the day before, and I give him checks to play with in return for gold dust. I seen him before once or twice, drinking at the bar or swamping out after the saloon was closed. I reckon that's how he earned his drinks."

"Objection!" The General stood, his face redder than usual. "Speculation!"

"Sustained," ruled Blair. "Strike that last remark from the record. The jury will disregard it." Crandall resumed his seat.

"Please continue, Mr. Shingle," Scout said.

"McCall started walking toward the back like he was fixing to go out the back door. Then he appeared to change his mind and turned around. I wasn't paying too much attention. About that time Bill and Cap'n Massey got into an argument over the game. I don't know what started it. It wasn't much of an argument, but they raised their voices some, and that's when I looked up and seen McCall fire his revolver.

"He fired from about two or three feet behind, saying, 'Take that.' The ball entered the back part of Wild Bill's head, and come out of the right cheek bone, entering the left wrist of Cap'n Massey. The shot killed Wild Bill instantly. He did not move and said nothing. He sat in the chair a couple of minutes and then fell over backward.

"McCall was moving toward the back door, with his revolver in his hand holding it up. As I went to look at Bill, McCall pointed the revolver at me and snapped it. I reckon it misfired or I wouldn't be here. But I wasn't taking no chances and got out of the house. The weapon used was a Sharps improved revolver, eighteen inches long, with a piece of buckskin sewed around the stock."

A heavy silence descended over the courtroom in the wake of the gold-dust weigher's narrative. The sudden squeal of hinges as the bailiff prepared to poke a fresh chunk of wood into the stove drew a startled gasp from the gallery. Scout waited another moment before asking his final question.

"Mr. Shingle, can you identify the man you saw shoot and kill James Butler Hickok?"

"That's him, sitting behind that table." He pointed at the man in shackles.

CHAPTER 5

"There are as many ways to approach a witness during cross-examination as there are lawyers," Bartholomew had once told Scout. "Some come barreling out from behind their tables, head down, like a bull buffalo challenging another for leadership of the herd. Others stroll around, their hands in their pockets, looking like they're interested in everything but the witness until the moment they dive for his jugular. Still others don't approach at all, preferring to fire barbed questions from their side of the table that ring in the rafters and keep the witness hopping from one subject to another with no chance to think before answering." General John Quincy Adams Crandall subscribed to none of these practices.

The rotund defense attorney got up from his seat slowly, as if answering a summons he would rather ignore, and strode to the witness box, where he placed his hands on the oaken rail and leaned forward, so that the gold-dust weigher was forced to sit up straight to avoid physical contact. This brought his hands up from where they had been dangling between his knees and he was faced once again with the problem of what to do with them. While he was fumbling, Crandall asked his first question.

"Mr. Shingle." He let the name hang there for a second, in the manner of a headmaster upbraiding an errant pupil. He sounded disappointed. "What are the dimensions of Saloon No. 10?"

Shingle's brow furrowed. "I would say it's about—"

"I didn't ask you what it was about. I asked for the dimensions." It came out harshly.

Scout considered objecting, but decided that it would serve no purpose. He wanted to see where the defender was heading.

"The room is twenty-four feet wide and twenty feet long. The bar is eight feet."

"Thank you. How many people were in the room at the time of the shooting?"

"Eight, counting me and Harry Young, the bartender."

"You mentioned that Hickok put down his shotgun when he joined the poker game. Did you notice if he was otherwise armed?"

The witness flashed a second nervous smile, in which the gold crown glinted. "Sure he was. That's like asking the king of Russia if he ever gets cold."

A guffaw went up from the gallery. Blair rapped for order.

Crandall's good-natured chuckle didn't reach his eyes. "What other weapons did he carry?"

"Well, he was packing them two ivory-handled Navies like always, stuck in a sash around his waist with the butts turned frontwise like for a cross draw, except he never crossed. He would twist his wrists to bring them out, like this." He demonstrated by curling both hands inside the skirt of his coat and swiveling them outward, bringing a brace of imaginary revolvers into play. "And then there was the derringers everyone knew he toted, one in each side pocket of his coat. Oh, and there was a bowie knife too, but I can't swear that he was wearing it that day."

"That's quite an arsenal. You said once that Hickok had at one time or another been an officer of the law. Was he acting in this capacity at the time of his death?"

Scout straightened. Why was Crandall pursuing a line he himself had objected to half an hour earlier?

"Well, sort of," replied the witness.

"Sort of?" The General had half-turned away. Now he swung around to face him once again. "Mr. Shingle, how do you 'sort of' enforce the law?"

Perspiration glistened on Shingle's rugged forehead. "Deadwood is a pretty new town. It don't exactly have no regular marshal. Folks generally looked to Wild Bill if there was any lawing to be done."

"Who appointed him to this position?"

"Well, no one, really. He just sort of started stepping in whenever there was trouble, him and his friends. Deputies, like."

"I see. He just started calling himself marshal and anyone who disagreed had to take it up with his friends, is that it?"

"Your Honor, I object most strenuously!" Scout was up and seething.

"Sustained. In the future, General, you will save such conclusions for your summation."

Crandall, still leaning on the rail before the witness box and staring at Shingle, appeared oblivious to the judge's rebuke for some seconds. Gradually he relaxed and straightened. "What sort of man was Wild Bill Hickok with a gun, Mr. Shingle?" he asked calmly.

The witness sat back, on solid ground once again. "Let me put it this way, Mr. Crandall," he said. "They didn't call him the Prince of Pistoleers for nothing."

"Did you ever see him in action?"

"Oh sure, lots of times. Bill was fond of showing off. One time in Hays City I seen him place five shots through the hole of an O on a sign a hundred paces across the street, then do the shift and place five more on top of the first five. He done it in less time than it takes to tell it. I never seen a man who could beat him except maybe Colorado Charlie Utter, and I don't believe Charlie ever had to shoot at a target that was shooting back, unless you count Indians and Johnny Rebs."

"Tell me, Mr. Shingle, how many men have you personally seen Hickok kill?"

"Objection!" roared Scout, springing to his feet. "Counsel for the defense is casting aspersions on a man who can no longer speak for himself. Furthermore, his entire line of questioning is irrelevant."

"Which is the only part of your objection that concerns us here," Blair informed him sternly. "However, I'm inclined to let it continue. You may proceed, General, but take care."

"Thank you, Your Honor. Well, Mr. Shingle? Shall I repeat the question?"

"No, sir." The gold-dust weigher had his handkerchief out and was mopping his face. "I only seen him kill one. It was in Hays City, when Jack Strawhan came gunning for him in Drum's saloon. I don't know why. Bill was county sheriff then, and was also filling in as city marshal. I was playing poker at a table in back. Bill was at the bar. Strawhan come in, seen Bill, and pulled out his pistol, but Bill beat him to it and shot him through the heart before he could squeeze off one round. I never seen anyone move as fast as Bill done that night."

"Do you have personal knowledge of any other killings committed by Hickok?"

"I know of Bill killing three men, but all in self-defense. He was tried and acquitted all three times."

"Then he had a reputation for speed and accuracy?"

"That's right."

Crandall had wandered away from the box and was now standing midway between it and the defense table with his back to Shingle. His hands were clasped behind his back and his eyes were on the opposite wall above the heads of the spectators. "Did you observe Hickok partake of alcoholic beverages the afternoon of his death?"

"Your Honor . . . !" complained the prosecutor.

"Is there a point to all this, General?" Blair asked.

"There is, Your Honor, if the court will bear with me a bit longer." Crandall had not turned around.

"I've already given you more time than conscience dictates. However . . ." The judge's voice trailed off.

The question was repeated. Shingle laughed shortly, but when there was no response from the gallery he resumed his customary grave expression. "If he wasn't drinking, I'd have known that the man pretending to be Wild Bill was an imposter."

"Why do you say that, Mr. Shingle?" The General was twirling the elk's tooth attached to his watch.

"He was a constant drinker. Wherever there was liquor to be found, there was where you would find Wild Bill." Hurriedly, as if he had divined suddenly where the interrogation was leading, he added, "But he was sober when this shooting occurred."

"Are you certain of that?"

"As sure as I am of how many checks an ounce of gold dust is good for."

Ponderously, Crandall turned to face the witness. When he spoke his voice shook the room.

"Mr. Shingle, are you suggesting that the man you knew as Wild Bill, an experienced killer with a speed and proficiency of firearms nearly unmatched in your experience, a man who valued his life so far as to prefer a seat against the wall with a view of both entrances, allowed his slayer to traverse twenty feet of open space in a nearly empty room, reverse directions, step up behind him, draw a revolver, announce his intentions with the words 'Take that!' and slam a bullet through his brain without raising so much as a finger to defend himself, even though he was stone cold sober and perfectly capable of doing so? Is that what you're suggesting, Mr. Shingle?"

Shingle was caught flat-footed. He sat bolt upright, opening and closing his mouth and gripping the wooden arms of his chair with big, white-knuckled hands. With a detachedness born of disaster, Scout mused that he seemed to have solved the problem of what to do with them.

"Bah!" Crandall exclaimed, casting the witness aside with a disgusted sweep of his arm. He stormed back to his seat.

"Redirect, Mr. Scout?" The judge's query was all but drowned out beneath the buzz of voices that came on the heels of Crandall's last question. He needn't have bothered. The prosecutor was already up and moving, anxious to kill his opponent's point before the jury had time to assimilate it.

"Deadwood is a wild, lawless place, Mr. Shingle." He had stopped in front of the box, where Shingle was busy employing the sodden handkerchief he had yet to return to his pocket. "You must have seen quite a few shootings from your table in the saloon."

"I seen my share." The witness' tone was suspicious. Whatever love he may have held for lawyers going into the courtroom had been dealt a fatal blow.

"In your opinion based on these observations and on what you saw on the afternoon of August second, did Wild Bill have a chance to defend himself against his assailant?"

"No, sir, he never did."

"Thank you. I have no more questions." Scout walked away.

Once dismissed, Shingle made for the exit as if bullets were splintering the floor at his heels.

"There's one gold-dust weigher who will never see another shooting," Bartholomew whispered gravely.

One of the items the court clerk had laid out on the judge's bench was a big railroad watch of age-darkened gold, its face left open. Blair glanced at it.

"Gentlemen," he announced, "it is only eleven-thirty. Rather than begin hearing new testimony, however, I suggest we break for lunch now. If there are no objections this court is adjourned until one o'clock." There were none. The gavel banged.

After the judge had retired to his chambers, the jurors were escorted by the bailiff to their room down the hall, where their meals

would be catered from the restaurant across the street. The defendant, who had sat motionless throughout the morning, staring at God
knew what—that crossed eye was misleading—presented the same
stony expression as he clanked out the side door flanked by two deputy U.S. marshals that he had on his way in. The gallery emptied
somewhat more slowly, but within a few minutes the four lawyers
were alone in the cavernous room. With a friendly nod to his opponents, the General gathered his papers into a brown leather portfolio
and left, leaning backward slightly as he negotiated the center aisle
to offset the forward pull of his paunch. Orville Gannon carried his
briefcase out behind his partner without so much as a glance in the
prosecutor's direction.

Bartholomew and Scout collected their overcoats from the cloak-
room and shrugged into them on their way down the broad staircase
to the ground floor. They stopped on the first landing while the prosecutor charged his pipe and his partner contemplated the contents of
his snuff box darkly. Shaking his head, the older attorney returned
the box to his vest pocket without partaking. "You picked up some
there at the end," he said.

"Not enough," growled Scout, around the pipe stem. They resumed the descent. "Were you watching the jury?"

"They had their eyes on Crandall most of the time, not a good
sign. But it's early yet. When they start watching the defendant
we'll know we've got them."

"That clever bastard, Crandall. Is he going for self-defense or
what?"

"Right now he's just muddying the waters. Forget about him and
concentrate on your case."

They had reached the lobby, brisk from the passage of many bod-
ies through the double doors that led to the street. Hundreds of
slushy footprints decorated the rubber mat just inside the entrance,
where a tall, middle-aged man in an old overcoat growing fuzzy at
the elbows spotted the newcomers and strode forward, drawing a
hand from his side pocket.

Scout stiffened, his mind flashing back to the near tragedy in the
restaurant last week. But the hand that was extended him proved to
be empty. He grasped it automatically and was astonished at the
power in the man's callused grip.

"Mr. Scout, I want you to know that there are folks who appreciate what it is you're trying to do," said the stranger.

The man's baritone was surprisingly gentle for the iron in his grasp and the craggy features that showed beneath the broad, weather-beaten brim of his hat. There was something familiar about him that the prosecutor was at a loss to identify.

"I'm sorry, do we know each other?"

The stranger laughed easily, showing tobacco-stained teeth behind a drooping brown moustache. "There I go again, forgetting to introduce myself," he said. "We don't get much chance to practice on the farm. I'm Lorenzo Hickok, Jim's brother. I been watching the proceedings."

Now Scout knew where he had seen him before, or rather his likeness. The hooked nose, gray eyes, and short chin were reminiscent of the rotogravures he had studied of James Butler Hickok. The features of both were dried and cracked from years of exposure to sun and wind, the latter's while scouting for the army on horseback and toiling in the gold fields around Deadwood, the former's while straining behind a plow on his mother's Illinois farm. This one looked to be about forty-five, which would make him an older brother. The prosecutor understood now the sudden rush of panic that had seized him at the stranger's approach; he had been reacting to the reputation of the other Hickok.

Scout introduced Bartholomew, who merely nodded, fiddling with his snuff box to avoid clasping hands. He had noted his partner's wince earlier.

"Have you come to give testimony?" asked the prosecutor.

Lorenzo Hickok shook his head once, shortly. "I wouldn't be much help. None of us has saw much of Jim since fifty-five, when he got in that fracas with Charley Hudson while they was working on the Illinois and Michigan canal and near killed him. He took off after that. Since then most of the news we got about him was what we seen in the papers and that *Harper's New Monthly* piece that come out about ten year ago. We was all right proud of him when we read that. All except Ma. She never did approve of anything Jim done after he left the farm.

"Anyway, we didn't hear he was dead until one of the neighbors showed it to my sister Celinda in the Chicago newspaper. She hid it in the kitchen and run down to the store to tell me and my brother

Horace. When we got back, there was Ma in the kitchen rocker with the paper in her lap, rocking away. Blood all down the front of her dress. She'd hemorrhaged. She ain't been the same since." His face was taut. "This time I come to see justice done."

"The state will do everything in its power to insure that it is," Scout told him, after a pause.

"I know that. I seen you trying just now."

"Don't be taken in by what you saw, Mr. Hickok. That was just the opening round."

Hickok said nothing at first. The expression in his gray eyes was right out of the pictures of his famous brother. "Well," he announced then, "I want you to know that if you need anything you won't have far to come. Us Hickoks stick together."

After Scout had noted the farmer's room number at a nearby hotel they stepped outside, where they parted on the top step. This time the prosecutor was prepared, and gave as good as he got during the final hand clasp. If it had any effect on Hickok, however, he didn't show it. He boarded a jitney down the block and was off in a spray of water and slush. The snow was two inches deep on the ground and still falling in large wet flakes.

"Sinister sort," said Bartholomew, adjusting his hat as he and Scout started across the street toward the restaurant.

"Wild Bill seems to have come by it honestly."

Inside the dining establishment, which was a small place unlike the scene of the prosecutor's recent adventure, the attorneys spotted Crandall and Gannon sharing a table in back and took refuge in a booth near the door. They had placed their orders when a boy in his late teens appeared at their table. He was wearing a gray uniform with brass buttons and carried an envelope.

"Mr. Scout?" He looked from one to the other.

The prosecutor jumped at the question. He had been knocking his pipe against an ashtray at his elbow and had not observed the boy's approach. "I'm Scout," he said, after a moment.

"Your office said you'd be here if you weren't in court." The envelope was extended.

Scout tipped him and broke the seal. The telegram had been dispatched from St. Paul, Minnesota at eleven o'clock that morning, and read:

AM ON MY WAY YANKTON STOP WILL BE THERE TOMORROW STOP
LOOKING FORWARD TO TESTIFYING ON BEHALF MY LATE FRIEND
WILD BILL STOP MY PRAYERS WITH YOU UNTIL THEN

WILLIAM FREDERICK CODY

The prosecutor flipped the wire to Bartholomew, who read it and frowned thoughtfully.

"Everyone's here but the Indians," he said.

CHAPTER 6

The state's second witness was Carl Mann, part owner of Saloon No. 10 and one of the men who had been playing poker with Hickok that fatal day. His testimony paralleled Shingle's closely, differing only over the weapon used, which he identified as "a Navy-size revolver." Scout hurried into his next question before the discrepancy, minor though it was, had a chance to sink into the jurors' minds and confuse them.

"Mr. Mann, would you tell us about the poker game that took place in the saloon the night before Hickok's death?"

Mann, heavy-set, ponderously moustached and balding, screwed up his face in thought. A wicked scar, years old, pulled down the outside corner of his left eyelid. When he spoke, his words came in short, nasty-sounding bursts that the prosecutor hoped wouldn't prejudice the jury against his statement.

"Wild Bill was playing when Jack McCall came in," he snapped. "McCall weighed out some gold dust to get some checks to play poker with Bill and others. McCall won twenty-three or twenty-four dollars, I'm not certain of the amount. He then went outdoors and came back and played again. Bill won and they came to the bar and asked me to weigh out twenty or twenty-five dollars. George Shingle had by this time gone home. Anyway, McCall's purse was short. Bill said, 'You owe me sixteen dollars and twenty-five cents.' McCall said, 'Yes,' and went out. He came back shortly after and Bill said, 'Did I break you?' McCall said, 'Yes.' Bill then gave him all the change he had, seventy-five cents, to buy his supper with and told him that if he, Bill, quit winner in the game he was playing he would give McCall more. McCall would not take the money and went out in fifteen or twenty minutes."

"Why do you suppose Bill was so generous?" Scout asked.

"Objection!" rapped Crandall. "Conjecture!" The judge sustained it.

The prosecutor remained unruffled. "Was Hickok in the habit of giving away part of his winnings?"

"Constantly. When he won, which he usually did," added the saloonkeeper. "Bill was like that."

"I see. How did McCall react to his offer? Was he grateful? Angry?"

"I would say angry."

"Resentful, perhaps?"

"Objection! Leading the witness!" The General's ruddy complexion took on a purplish tinge.

"The witness has already answered the question, counselor," Blair reminded Scout.

"I'm sorry, Your Honor. No more questions."

"You said that Hickok was accustomed to surrendering a portion of his spoils," Crandall began, when his opponent had returned to his seat. He was leaning back against the defense table, hands buried deep in his pants pockets. "What was his attitude on these occasions? Expansive?"

"That is not the word I would use, sir," Mann replied. He had crossed his legs and inserted his thumbs inside his vest pockets. His gaze met Crandall's and remained steady.

"What word would you use, Mr. Mann?"

" 'Overbearing' strikes me as appropriate."

"Objection!" Scout stood. "I fail to see what this has to do with the case at hand."

Crandall spread his hands with a bewildered smile. "I am merely exploring an area opened up by counsel for the prosecution, Your Honor."

"He's right, Mr. Scout. Overruled."

As he sat down fuming, the prosecutor glanced at McCall, now staring intently at the man on the stand. For the first time he seemed to be taking an interest in the proceedings.

" 'Overbearing,' Mr. Mann?" Crandall pressed. "How so?"

The saloonkeeper smirked, clearly relishing his moment in the sun. "When he had cleaned someone out, and especially when he had been drinking heavily, he would puff himself up like a rooster and flip a check at the loser. He didn't mean to be humiliating, understand—he just liked to play the big butter-and-egg man. But that was the result."

"Was this his posture the night he offered Mr. McCall seventy-five cents and indicated that more might follow?"

"Yes, sir, it was."

"Thank you, Mr. Mann."

Scout was caught off guard by the General's abrupt conclusion. He had expected the defender to challenge Mann's testimony regarding the shooting, or at least to bring up the matter of the type of revolver used. As it was, the prosecutor had barely got himself settled in his seat when his opponent went back to his own table. Blair was surprised too. There was a pause before the judge asked Scout if he cared to redirect. The prosecutor declined. Mann stepped down.

"What was that about?" Scout whispered to his partner. Bartholomew shook his head. He looked worried.

Captain William Rodney Massey was tall and well built, and as he approached the stand his rolling gait bespoke his extensive experience as a steamboat pilot on the Missouri River. Middle-aged, he appeared younger, with dark, wavy hair untouched by gray and a chestnut rectangle of beard not connected to his burnsides, adding length to his face. He wore a suit of an expensive cut not often found this far west. A solitary feminine sigh came from somewhere in the gallery when he turned around to be sworn in. Scout noted that he seemed to be making a favorable impression upon the all-male jury as well, a difficult feat for an attractive man.

Under Scout's questioning, the witness stated that he had been among the gamblers at Hickok's table on the second, but that he had not seen the shooting itself. "I was looking down at the table when the pistol report came," he said quietly. "I felt a shock and numbness in my left wrist and looked up to see the defendant backing toward the rear door, saying, 'Come on, you sons of bitches.' I got out quick as I could and did not see Wild Bill fall. I looked up at the pistol and my eyes passed him. The ball was not found on examination of my arm. It is there yet, I suppose."

"Had you ever seen the defendant before that afternoon?" asked the prosecutor.

"Yes, I did. I saw the defendant come into the same room a day or two before and walk around behind Bill and pull his pistol about two thirds out. There was a young man with him who put his arm around the defendant and walked him toward the back door."

The spectators began buzzing. Blair rapped gently. When it was quiet again Scout asked Massey a few more questions to fix the details of the shooting, then turned him over to Crandall. The General approached the witness box on cat's feet, as if he suspected a Confederate battery were concealed inside.

"Do you consider yourself an observant man, Captain Massey?"

The seated man smiled faintly behind his beard. "The number of small craft which ply the Missouri make a certain amount of watchfulness necessary," he replied.

"It would appear so, since you seem to be the only person in existence who saw Mr. McCall draw a weapon on Wild Bill a day or two before his death."

"Objection." Scout kept his seat. "Is counsel for the defense making his summation at this time?"

"Sustained," said the judge. "You've been warned, General."

Crandall apologized. His eyes never left the witness. "Are you conversant in firearms weaponry, Captain Massey?"

"Well, I do not qualify as an expert, but I am in the habit of carrying a side arm and fancy that I know one end of it from the other."

"I'm afraid I don't understand, Captain." The defense counsel sounded genuinely puzzled. "You say that you are observant and that you are no stranger to firearms, but if both these things are true then I fear that you are guilty of perjury. Are you aware of the penalties for lying under oath, Captain Massey?"

Scout was up in a flash. "Your Honor, this is character assassination!"

"Is that an objection, Mr. Scout?"

"It is, Your Honor," he replied, flustered.

Blair turned to Crandall. "This is a serious charge, General. Can you back it up?"

"I can, if Your Honor will direct the court recorder to read back Captain Massey's answer to Mr. Scout's first question regarding the shooting."

The judge nodded to the young man at the writing desk, who paged back through his notes and began reading in an emotionless monotone:

" 'I was looking down at the table when the pistol report came. I felt a shock and numbness in my left wrist—' "

"Go ahead a few lines, please," requested Crandall.

" 'I got out quick as I could and did not see Wild Bill fall,' " the recorder continued. " 'I looked up at the pistol and my eyes passed him. The ball—' "

"That will be enough, thank you." The General turned back to Massey. "Captain Massey, are you aware of the difference between a revolver and a pistol?"

The pilot smiled in obvious relief, white teeth flashing in the dark beard. "Oh, that. Well, I was merely indulging in an expression."

Crandall's head snapped around to the bench. "Will Your Honor please direct the witness to answer the question?"

Blair did so, trying to conceal a smile. He had seen where the defender was heading.

"Of course I am aware of the difference," said Massey, nettled. "A revolver is equipped with a cylinder and can fire up to six times without reloading. A pistol is a single-shot and has no cylinder."

"Captain, two other witnesses have testified that a revolver was employed in the shooting. They can't seem to agree on what type it was"—he glanced wryly toward the jury—"but at least they are of one mind that it was a revolver. You are the only one who has identified it as a pistol, just as you alone claim to have seen the defendant produce a weapon in the saloon before August second. Since you have demonstrated your knowledge of the difference between a pistol and a revolver, I can only assume that somewhere you are lying. Or is it that you are not as observant as you think? That you cannot be sure that you saw what you think you saw on either occasion? Or were you drunk? Answer me, Captain Massey; were you drunk the day you claim to have seen my client make an aborted attempt on Hickok's life?"

"Objection!" cried Scout, springing from his seat.

"*Answer the question*, Captain!" Crandall was shouting, his face inches from Massey's. The pilot, his countenance now nearly as red as that of his tormentor, seemed on the verge of striking him and had half-risen from his chair to brace himself. The bailiff started forward from his position against the wall.

"Objection! Objection! My opponent is badgering the witness!"

Scout was almost shrieking, half in anger, half in fear that his witness would make good on his unspoken threat.

"General Crandall!" Blair nearly cracked the handle of his gavel pounding it. "You cannot expect a man to answer a question until you give him a chance. Captain Massey, please sit down."

After a tense moment the pilot lowered himself back into his seat, glaring at Crandall. Savagely he swept back a lock of hair that had tumbled forward over his brow. The bailiff returned to his post but remained wary.

"The witness is directed to answer the question," said the judge.

"It's all right, Your Honor," Crandall said, sounding pleased with himself. "I withdraw the question."

"But not the taint," Scout muttered, not quite under his breath.

"What was that, counselor?" snapped the judge.

"Nothing, Your Honor."

"I will have no more of these asides. Proceed, General."

You had to hand it to Crandall, Scout thought, hating him. Rather than release the witness for redirect in time for Scout to remove the doubts he had planted in the jury's mind about Massey's reliability before they took root, the General spent another ten minutes asking for such things as a fresh description of the barroom and its occupants, knowing that any objections raised by the prosecutor would only delay things further. By the time Scout was allowed to ask the question his opponent had deliberately left hanging, Massey's assurance that he had not been imbibing heavily at the time of either incident made no impression whatever. Crandall had succeeded in weakening the thickest part of the state's fence.

When the prosecutor started back toward his table after finishing with Captain Massey, Bartholomew smiled at him reassuringly, as if he had divined his partner's thoughts. At times like this he reminded Scout of a favorite and rather dotty old uncle. Taking courage from this, he turned and caught the judge's eye.

"Your Honor, the state's next witness will signal a new phase of its case, which will demand this court's complete and undivided attention. If there are no objections on the part of my distinguished colleague, I therefore request that we adjourn until tomorrow morning after all parties involved have had a night's rest."

"General?" Blair asked.

"No objections, Your Honor."

"This court is adjourned until nine o'clock tomorrow morning." The gavel banged.

"Don't make anything more of Crandall's attack than it is," Bartholomew told Scout when they were in front of the courthouse waiting for a cab. It had stopped snowing and dusk had begun to gather over rooftops cloaked in white. "We've lost a day or two of premeditation, that's all."

"He's got to be going for self-defense." A cab was rattling toward them. The man at the reins, whose face was a cherry-red strip between a gray woolen muffler and his lowered hat brim, pulled in at Scout's signal. The prosecutor started and backed away as a passenger he hadn't noticed unfolded his lanky frame from the seat and got down to pay the driver. The man's apology was perfunctory and tinted with a faint southern accent. He then strode briskly up the steps to the door of the court building, leaving Scout with the fleeting image of slim features vague in the failing light and a costly suit and overcoat either brand new or freshly pressed.

"Eight to five he's on his way up to see you," said Bartholomew, boarding. "There'll be time enough for that tomorrow if he's anxious. Do you have plans for the evening?"

Scout looked at him ruefully. "If I did, they've just been changed. I've a feeling we'll be burning a lot of oil tonight."

They were two blocks from Scout's second-floor apartment dwelling before Bartholomew spoke again. "All right, what is it?"

"What's what?" His partner was watching the scenery.

"You've been skittish as a filly all day. Lorenzo Hickok, that boy with the telegram, and that passenger just now had you jumping. Something's happened I don't know about. Now, what is it?"

Scout looked at him, sighed, and handed him a folded sheet he had taken from an inside pocket. "That was under the office door when I got in this morning. I didn't want to bother you with it. I figured it was just a crank, but it's been on my mind ever since."

The older attorney unfolded the note and read it. It was pieced together from letters clipped from a newspaper, and threatened Scout's life if he didn't drop the case against Jack McCall.

CHAPTER 7

"I thought you'd gone out."

Dora Hope, in her dressing gown, dark hair arranged in a braid draped over her right shoulder, was standing in front of the parlor door when her daughter came in from the veranda. Grace Sargent was wearing her black gown and a fur hat to match her stole and muff. She smiled in spite of her disappointment. "Julian had to change his plans," she replied. "He came to say he's working tonight and to apologize."

"That McCall case, I suppose. Well, if hanging a man is more important to him than you are . . ." She left it at that.

"Don't start, Mother."

Upstairs, undressing for bed, Grace thought about the conversation she had just had with Julian and was glad she hadn't told her mother about the man she had seen watching them from the shadows beyond the street lamp on the corner.

"That's my bodyguard," Julian had said shamefacedly when she clutched his sleeve and pointed. "He's a deputy U.S. marshal. Tessie insisted on borrowing him from Burdick after that fiasco the other night. He's a blasted nuisance."

He had assured her that he was in no danger, and so she said nothing more about it. But she knew there was more to it than what he had told her. Julian's partner was level-headed in spite of his idiosyncrasies (Mother, disapproving of his snuff-taking, refused to have him in the house) and would not panic over an incident as foolish as the restaurant confrontation. Of course, given his ambitions, there was a bare possibility that he hoped to use the danger angle later as a political tool, but she doubted that even he was shrewd enough to be able to turn a belligerent drunk into a threat that would display his partner's courageous sense of duty.

Not telling her mother about the drunk had led to an ugly scene when it appeared in the Yankton newspaper. By the time Grace related their side of the story, Mrs. Hope had already been influenced by the press distortion; she ordered her daughter to stop seeing Julian, to which Grace replied hotly that she would take no orders, and a shouting match had ensued. They had only just begun speaking to each other again. Grace shuddered to think what her mother's reaction would be if she learned that Julian had engaged a bodyguard, like a gambling czar or a dishonest politician.

Now, seated on the edge of her mattress in her chemise, removing her stockings, Grace decided that she couldn't blame her mother for acting the way she had. It was Mother who had found Edgar the night the household was awakened by shooting, crumpled on the threshold of the open front door seconds after the killer had fled. Edgar always audited his own books late into the evening to make sure his bookkeepers weren't stealing from him, and had apparently answered the door after everyone else had retired, collecting three bullets for his trouble. He had lived just long enough to describe his assailant to a deputy town marshal who rode with him to the hospital. The killer, a young man from Massachusetts who had lost everything when work on the Great Northern Pacific Railroad had shut down, was found two nights later hanging from a ceiling beam in his quarters at a city boarding house, evidently a suicide.

The tragedy had had a profound effect on Mother, though not the one Grace might have expected. She had developed a sudden morbid interest in violence and death, and had begun subscribing to several newspapers in which she read only those items relating to brutal crimes. Tragedy itself held a fascination for her, and though with casual acquaintances she professed a ladylike disregard for the subject, when alone with Grace she would discuss at length the details of some lurid murder that had found its way into the columns. Alarmed, Grace had persuaded a doctor to visit on a pretense and inveigle Mrs. Hope into a conversation upon her favorite topic, to determine her sanity. After an hour the doctor had taken his leave. Meeting with Grace later, he had told her that there was nothing to worry about, that her mother's condition was temporary and had been brought on by shock over the manner of her son-in-law's death. That had been two years ago, and murder was still very much on Dora Hope's mind.

The subject lost its appeal, however, whenever the conversation became personal. She would not discuss Edgar's murder, and when Grace, confronted with the item describing Julian's "brawl," had told her of the other man's attempt to draw a revolver, Mother had become hysterical. It was at times like this that Grace realized that the fence her mother had constructed around herself was made of brittle glass, easily shattered.

It's this house, she thought. If she could get Mother to leave it, she was certain that in time she would come to accept what had happened to Edgar and abandon her sinister hobby. But none of the prospective buyers would meet Mother's price, and she was determined not to let it go for anything less than it was worth. This stubbornness was pure Dora Hope, a holdover from the days when she had to make every penny count, and had nothing to do with her mental disturbance. But the house was killing her.

Short of finding a buyer, the only thing that would tear Mother away from that mausoleum was if Julian married Grace and she came to live with them. She was fiercely protective, and since her maternal instincts were stronger than her parsimony, her daughter felt sure that she would leave the mansion without a qualm if separation was the alternative. That was why Grace had been so disappointed the other night when the inebriate had interrupted just as Julian seemed about to propose.

Or was that the reason? True, the attorney held a strong attraction for her, but then she had felt just as strongly about Edgar, and that had not been a good marriage. In fact, she had been contemplating divorce at the time of his death. Love was something she had yet to experience, if indeed it existed at all. But if she didn't love Julian, why was she using her mother's welfare as an excuse to marry him, when she could accomplish the same thing simply by moving out, knowing that Mother would follow whether she had a husband or not? She sighed, disgusted with herself. At thirty she was no more sure of her emotions than she had been at sixteen.

She paused before donning her nightgown to regard her reflection in the mirror atop the bureau. She was attractive if not quite beautiful, and her figure was as appealing naked as it was when bedecked in the whalebone and steel contraptions women employed in search of social acceptance. Her breasts were full and her waist was tiny without artificial aid, and if her shoulders seemed a bit too square, they were balanced by the swell of her hips. Her thighs, plump and round the way men seemed to prefer them (judging by the glimpse she had once got of a painted nude as she was passing a saloon), tapered to well-shaped calves and trim ankles and small, perfect feet. The freckles on her face and breasts were something she had learned to live with. Yes, she decided as she slipped the nightgown on over her head, Julian would get around to proposing yet. And she knew what her answer would be.

As she crawled shivering beneath the counterpane—she kept no fire in her room—Grace was prepared for a long wait before falling asleep. She wasn't accustomed to retiring this early. Scarcely had she turned down her bedside lamp and turned over, however, before she felt herself drifting off. Her last conscious thought was that soul-searching appeared to be an excellent cure for insomnia.

The man watching from a doorway across the street waited a full five minutes after he had seen the light go off in the second-story window before moving. Huddled there with his hat pulled low and his collar turned up against the icy wind, he had felt his pulse quicken as Grace Sargent's shadow fell across the lattice. He had wanted her right then, but with the servants and the old lady, there were too many in the house. The trial had just started and there would be other nights.

Fearing that he had been spotted, he had been alarmed earlier when Julian Scout had shown up at the house accompanied by one of Marshal Burdick's deputies, but when both left together it was evident that the prosecutor was the one being protected and not his woman. The watcher suspected that the message his partner had had him deliver was responsible for that. He made a mental note to remember to call him Smith whenever anyone else was within earshot.

When he was certain that she had gone to bed and was not gazing out the window the way women sometimes did, he left the shelter of the doorway and started for home and a drink. Jesus, but it was cold.

Flames gulped greedily of the logs in the grate, driving the chill dampness from the office shared by the prosecution team. Disgusted with sluggish bureaucracy, Scout and Bartholomew had chipped in to have the flue repaired, and now the chimney was drawing like sixty for the first time in two years. Scout, in shirtsleeves and vest, used the tongs to extract a glowing ember and lit his pipe.

"Where is justice when a roomful of eyewitnesses can't convict a man of cold-blooded murder?" he snarled, flinging the ember back into the hearth. "If this were New York, McCall would have dropped through the trap weeks ago."

At his desk, Bartholomew was unstrapping the briefcase he seldom carried, a handsome one of black leather with gold corners. "You just answered your own question," he said. "Death by violence is nothing unusual out here, and so it must be broken down into categories before justice can take over. I didn't think I had to tell you that."

"All the same, I'd feel better if we could put a handle on Crandall's case."

"That was obvious from the minute Blair struck down his motion for acquittal on the grounds of double jeopardy. In order to build up McCall's character, he'll have to tear down Hickok's." From the briefcase he extracted a voluminous stack of yellowed newspaper clippings and bound periodicals, which he deposited atop the freshly cleared desk with a resounding thud. Curls of dust issued from between the pages.

"What's all that?" Scout asked, approaching the pile.

"Our case." The older attorney picked up the top item, a bound volume half an inch thick, and tossed it to his partner, who clapped it to his chest with both hands.

It was a copy of *Harper's New Monthly Magazine* for February 1867. Scout donned his reading glasses and opened it to the frontispiece, a full-length engraving of a long-haired man in frontier garb, one hand resting on the butt of a side arm strapped around his knee-length coat. It was captioned: WILD BILL. Scout flipped through the pages, stopping to read here and there. One passage read:

> There was a few seconds of that awful stillness, and then there was a dead silence. I put down the rifle and took the revolver, and said to myself: "Only six shots and nine men to kill. Save your powder, Bill, for the death-hug's a-comin'!"

The text was sprinkled with illustrations: Wild Bill defending himself with a bowie knife against a roomful of ruffians; Wild Bill on horseback, swimming a river to escape a regiment of Confederate soldiers; Wild Bill calmly allowing himself to be "put upon" at a game of poker; Wild Bill wheeling to point his six-shooter at a cowering group of desperadoes after killing their friend in an armed face-off in the street. The prosecutor looked up at his partner with a pained expression.

"This is a whitewash!"

"So is all this," agreed the other, indicating the rest of the material on the desk. "Except for some diatribes against him, which are just as naïve. I've been gathering the stuff ever since you were assigned to the case. I'd never realized how much had been written about Hickok until I started."

"We can't use this! Crandall will tear it apart!"

"Most of it, yes. But some of it's bound to stick. We'll keep him so busy attacking Wild Bill he won't have time to defend his client."

"You're the one who's always saying that it's the prosecutor's job to simplify, not complicate."

"It's Hickok versus McCall. What could be simpler?"

Scout sucked noisily on his pipe, thinking fiercely. "What makes you think Blair will allow it?"

"He already has. He opened the door today when he let the General question Carl Mann about that 'overbearing' comment."

"I don't like it."

"Julian, do you want to win this case?"

"Objection," Scout said, smiling slowly. "Leading the witness."

Bartholomew returned the smile, then flicked a finger at the periodical in his partner's hands. "Who gets the armchair tonight?"

In the corridor outside the office, the man wearing a deputy's star smoked and watched the staircase leading up from the floor below.

CHAPTER 8

Bartholomew groaned when he spotted the man he had come to meet at the station the next morning.

In the crowd on the platform he stood out, tall, well built, the famous dark brown tresses cascading over his shoulders, his clean profile set off by a modest handlebar and a spray of chin whiskers adding purpose to a jaw that had been sturdy to begin with. At thirty he was already an impressive figure, but the effect was spoiled by the flamboyance of his dress. A shirt of bleached doeskin with a fringed hem hung skirtlike below his knees, decorated with intricate beadwork and cinched at the waist by a belt with a big square buckle. A gold band encircled the tall crown of his white Stetson. In spite of the freezing weather he had his coat, a fine one of chamois leather with a fur lining, folded over one forearm as if he thought wearing it might detract from his costume. The outfit was designed to impress gullible Easterners and the kind of people that hung around railroad stations waiting to see who had come in on the train. When the time came to testify, Bartholomew knew that such gaucherie would elicit only contempt from the jury box. The man was a walking lethal cross-examination.

"Cody!" hailed the attorney, waving. "Colonel Cody!"

William Frederick Cody—Buffalo Bill—was busy describing for a knot of admirers the battle of Rawhide Creek, in which he had slain the Cheyenne sub-chief, Yellow Hand, and captured his warbonnet and scalp last July. Already a household name at the time of the encounter, Cody had since turned his fresh notoriety into a series of profitable personal appearances back East and was preparing a drama that would employ the headdress and cured trophy as props. He looked up in irritation as his name was called.

"Mr. Scout?"

"Bartholomew," corrected the other, accepting the great man's handshake. His grip was strong and his palm callused despite the manicure. "This is a very great honor indeed."

Cody waved aside the compliment with an expansive gesture, but the attorney noted a gleam he had seen in women's eyes when acknowledging a flattery.

"A thousand miles is a small price to pay to avenge a friend." The reply was delivered with an easy, rumbling cadence that made Bartholomew suspect that it had been rehearsed on board the train. He was suddenly aware that everyone on the platform was watching them, and for the first time since his initial court appearance thirty years ago he felt embarrassed.

"I've a cab waiting at the end of the platform," he said hastily. "Are those your bags?" He lunged for the handle of an expensive valise standing beside a carpetbag at the famous scout's patent-leather feet.

"The porter will take care of them." Flipping what looked like a five-dollar gold piece to a black man in uniform, Cody struck out in the direction indicated by the attorney, unraveling the crowd as he went. Bartholomew noticed that most of those who hastened to keep up with him were men scribbling in dog-eared notepads with stubby pencils. Reporters, thought the attorney darkly. Neither he nor Scout had notified the press of Cody's anticipated arrival. The damned popinjay must have wired the newspapers at the same time he wired Scout.

His account of the battle finished by the time they reached the cab, Buffalo Bill ignored the journalists' further questions while his luggage was being loaded into the compartment. Gratefully, Bartholomew reflected that neither of the bags was large enough to accommodate any more theatrical getups without risk of damage.

"That's all, gentlemen," announced Cody as the wheels began to roll. "Any further statements concerning my friendship with Wild Bill will be made under oath."

Bartholomew gave the driver the name of the hotel where Cody told him he had a reservation, and settled back into the cold leather seat. He thought about snuff but decided against it. Lately he wondered how he had acquired the habit when the opportunity to partake presented itself so rarely. He supposed that he was getting respectable in his old age.

"Bracer, Mr. Bartholomew?"

The attorney blinked at the hammered silver flask thrust beneath his nose. The odor of whiskey stung his nostrils. Caught by surprise, he shook his head. Cody shrugged, withdrew the vessel, and put it to his own lips, tipping it expertly.

"That takes the place of a good overcoat anytime," he said, touching his lips with the back of his hand. He helped himself to a second, shorter swig and returned it, corked, to the pocket of the coat draped across his lap. Bartholomew agreed that it had its merits and helped himself to a healthy pinch of snuff.

"Your decision to testify was a most pleasant surprise, Colonel Cody." He carefully avoided phrasing it as a question, conscious of how much that would make him sound like one of the reporters they had just left.

He anticipated a bombastic reply typical of the star of "Scouts of the Prairie," but was moved when the great man said quietly, "I was well into my eastern tour when I learned of Wild Bill's murder. The weight upon my heart has been heavy enough of late without adding the burden of a friend unavenged."

As he spoke, Cody watched Yankton roll past the cab, either not caring or unwilling to meet the attorney's gaze. Bartholomew knew that Cody's six-year-old son had succumbed to scarlet fever last spring. He found himself wondering about this man who a scant eleven years ago had been a Union private still in his teens, but who had since been awarded the Congressional Medal of Honor for valor under fire, hunted buffalo for the Union Pacific, become the hero of a line of penny dreadfuls drafted by Edward Z. C. Judson under the pen name of Ned Buntline, appeared in a blushingly laudatory drama about his life on the plains, and still found time to scout for the army, fight Indians, and escort Russia's Grand Duke Alexis on a State Department-sponsored "safari" in quest of buffalo. In his time the attorney had defended men who would literally have eaten one such as this for breakfast; yet he fascinated him. The man's personality was overwhelming. Bartholomew couldn't help thinking what a politician he'd make.

"When do I appear?" Cody was looking at him.

The attorney realized that he had been staring at his companion. He sneezed into his handkerchief. "Tomorrow morning," he said, wiping his nose. "Just before the state rests its case."

"Won't that be rather late?"

"The timing should be perfect. Julian—Mr. Scout—and I were up until dawn researching what's been written about your friendship with Hickok, and we've come to the conclusion that you are the one most qualified to testify concerning his character."

"What about his widow? I'm told he married shortly before his death."

"He and Agnes Thatcher Lake were wed only two weeks when he left to seek his fortune in Deadwood. She knows rather less about him than the average reader of dime novels back East." He stopped short, remembering Ned Buntline.

Cody was unoffended. He sat back, blowing out his moustache thoughtfully. "I seem to be the man upon whom the entire case stands or falls."

Bartholomew steered a cautious course through that one. "McCall's lawyer is a crafty old warhorse. We aren't sparing the ar-tillery."

"I am not a man of words, but of action," said the other, his pom-posity returning. "Nevertheless you may assure your partner that with his guidance—and yours—I shall do everything in my power to see that justice prevails."

His pledge was so much like Scout's promise to Hickok's brother that the attorney could think of nothing to say in response. They rode for some time after that in silence, Cody studying Yankton's bleak winter-clad scenery, Bartholomew weighing his companion's words to determine how much was truth and how much idle fustian. He decided to take a chance.

"Colonel Cody," he began uneasily, "about your clothes . . ."

The jury was out of the room when Bartholomew returned to court, having seen Buffalo Bill safely to his quarters. Both Scout and Crandall were at the bench, gesturing agitatedly, their voices an angry murmur. The gallery was silent, straining to hear what was being said. Orville Gannon, writing at the defense table, appeared oblivious to everything, while the defendant sat staring stoically at the floor between the table and the bench. There was no one on the stand.

"Gentlemen, gentlemen," Blair was saying, his voice ragged with tension, "this bickering will accomplish nothing. As for you, Gen-eral, your language has brought you as close to a contempt-of-court citation as you are ever likely to come and remain free. Your objection is overruled. The publication introduced by the state will be introduced as evidence relating to the deceased's character."

"Your Honor, I request an exception." Crandall's tone was hot.

"It will be noted."

"Since the bench is determined to go through with this, I must also request a recess until tomorrow morning to allow Mr. Gannon and myself time to prepare a rebuttal to Mr. Scout's—evidence."

"Have you the material necessary for such a rebuttal?"

"We have, Your Honor. In my office."

"Where is your office, counselor?"

"Just around the corner, Your Honor, two flights up from the street."

"In that case you have twenty minutes."

"Twenty minutes! Your Honor, that is hardly enough—"

"General Crandall." Blair sounded grim. "I am familiar with your record as an attorney and with your tactics, and I remind you that this court's case load will not permit any unnecessary delays. You have twenty minutes. Make the most of them." The gavel cracked like a pistol shot.

"What happened?" Bartholomew whispered, when he and Scout had regained their seats. No one else had left his, except for the judge, who had withdrawn to his chambers, and Crandall, who had stalked out ostensibly in quest of the aforementioned material. Gannon continued writing.

"Nothing we didn't expect," replied the prosecutor, sounding as if he had been enjoying himself. "After that jailer Robinson testified on McCall's November escape attempt I whipped out that copy of *Harper's* and Crandall raised hell. I argued that McCall's defense had questioned Hickok's character and that I was merely using a national journal to rebut. Crandall said that it was not a sworn document. I responded that the state would produce a witness later who would confirm the essentials. When Blair ordered the jury withdrawn to let us slug it out I knew we had him. Once you peel away that smooth veneer, the General's temper is uncontrollable. I played on that."

"Just don't push him too far. A recess while he cools his heels in jail could hurt us."

"You're the one who taught me how to bring someone to the brink and leave him teetering."

"I also taught you to make sure you know which way the wind is blowing first."

The comment irritated Scout. "What are you most worried about, my losing this case or ruining your chances to put me in office?"

Bartholomew's head jerked backward as if recoiling from a physical blow. Ashamed for his outburst, the prosecutor was about to apologize when his partner lashed out in a vicious whisper: "Who told you that, your rich lady friend?" His face was distorted.

"Leave her out of this, Tessie."

The warning, delivered in a low murmur, made the older attorney back off. "It's a shaky point," he said, returning to the original subject. "I'm surprised Crandall didn't call for a declaration of mistrial on the grounds of bench prejudice."

It took Scout a moment to adjust to the swift change. Then he shook his head. "Blair would just deny it, and then where would he be? A prejudiced magistrate is better than a hostile one. Anyway, he knows Blair isn't prejudiced, just in a hurry to finish. We've got Crandall backed into a corner."

"Which is when he's most dangerous."

It was Scout's turn to change the subject. The flare-up, their first while a trial was in progress, had unsettled him. He hadn't realized that the animosity between his partner and his future intended went so deep. "Did you get our witness settled in?"

"When I left him he was in the middle of a flurry of clerks and bellhops. They made less fuss in St. Paul when President Grant visited."

"We're pinning a lot on him. What kind of impression do you think he'll make?"

"He'll make an impression; count on it."

General Crandall came puffing into the courtroom just as Blair was reaching for his gavel; he was lugging a stack of dusty documents as thick as Bartholomew's own under one arm. Asked by the judge if he was ready to proceed, he replied that he was, upon which the gavel descended and Scout rose with the copy of *Harper's* open to the first page of the article about Wild Bill.

" 'Several months after the ending of the Civil War,' " he read, " 'I visited the city of Springfield in southwest Missouri. Springfield is not a burgh of extensive dimensions, yet it is the largest in that part of the state, and all roads lead to it—which is one reason why it was the *point d'appui,* as well as the base of operations for all military movements during the war. . . .'"

Quoting from the journal, the prosecutor described the writer's introduction to Wild Bill during his stay in Springfield, repeating what Hickok had told him of his adventures. He related Bill's experiences as an espionage agent and sharpshooter for the Union, his victory single-handed over nine armed members of the McCanles gang in defense of Nebraska's Rock Creek Station in 1861, his 1865 winning fast-draw battle against Dave Tutt in Springfield, ending in the latter's death. For support he called upon information contained in other publications, which were also tagged as evidence over Crandall's objections, and used them to bring other incidents to light, among them Hickok's famous duel with Phil Coe while serving as city marshal of Abilene, Kansas, five years ago:

"'Trouble between Wild Bill and Coe had been brewing for some time over the unwholesome activities going on beneath the roof of Thompson and Coe's Bull's Head Saloon,'" he said, reading from a yellowed and brittle newspaper clipping. "'Wild Bill had directed Coe on several occasions to "clean up" his business "or answer to me," and had collected only abuse in return, which he accepted with his customary equanimity. On the night of October 5 a drunken row broke out at First Street and Cedar, in the course of which a shot was fired. Wild Bill came charging out of the Alamo Hotel, demanding to know who had discharged a firearm within the city limits.

"'Coe, his pistol still in hand, informed him sneeringly that he had just shot a dog "and am fixing to shoot another." But before he could fire, Bill drew his own weapon and a volley ensued. One ball passed between the marshal's limbs, another dislodged his hat from his head. One man in the crowd was killed and two others were wounded, probably by Coe's hand. Bill struck Coe in the groin with his last ball, injuring him fatally.'"

Finishing, Scout cast a sidelong glance at the jury and was pleased to see that they had been hanging on every word. Hickok's bravery and sense of duty were firmly established.

"Instructions, Your Honor," said Crandall, shattering the mood. "Since one cannot cross-examine a document, may I question counsel for the prosecution?"

Blair pursed his lips. With his bluish complexion the expression made him look like a fish. "It's highly irregular," he responded finally, "but then so is this entire chain of evidence. Unless Mr. Scout has objections I'll direct the bailiff to administer the oath."

"That won't be necessary, Your Honor." The General gestured expansively. "My colleague seems an honorable man."

"Your faith is heartening, counselor," said the judge, "but procedure will be followed. Mr. Scout?"

"No objections, Your Honor."

"Very well. Bailiff."

Once the prosecutor was sworn in, Crandall left him sitting in the box while he strolled over to the broad rail before the jury where the documents had been deposited, and studied them page by page. The idea, Scout knew, was to make him nervous. The gallery was becoming restless and Blair was fingering his gavel when Crandall finally spoke. He was leaning with his not inconsiderable backside supported against the rail and held the newspaper clipping in one hand.

"It appears, Mr. Scout, that you did not read the entire account of the duel in Abilene."

"Newspaper accounts are often wordy," Scout said calmly. "I read what I thought was applicable."

Crandall approached him. "We'll leave what is and is not applicable to the bench, if you don't mind. Your Honor?" He handed the clipping up to Blair, who put on his spectacles and pored over the item for the second time, frowning. At length he returned it.

"Proceed, counselor."

"Thank you, Your Honor." The General extended the clipping to the man in the box. "Would you mind reading from where you left off, Mr. Scout?"

Scout studied his opponent's face for a moment before replying. Teeth showed at the corners of his benevolent smile. "Not at all," said the prosecutor, accepting the scrap.

"'. . . Bill struck Coe in the groin with his last ball, injuring him fatally. But one of his earlier shots had killed Wild Bill's own friend Mike Williams, who had come to his aid, and whom Bill had mistaken for an enemy. The marshal had been so quick on the trigger that he had not had time to distinguish friend from foe.'"

The spectators buzzed. Crandall fired his next question before

Blair could wield his gavel. "Mr. Scout, have you any reason to doubt this newspaper's veracity?"

Scout smiled at him ruefully. "I'd be a fool to do so after entering it as evidence, now wouldn't I, counselor?"

"The witness is instructed to answer the question," said the judge. "I have no reason for doubt."

"Don't you find it odd that a man 'so quick on the trigger' as to shoot down a friend by mistake would not lift a finger to defend himself when his life was really at stake, as in Saloon No. 10?"

"Objection," said Scout. "Leading the witness."

"Sustained. Rephrase the question, General."

"I withdraw it, Your Honor." Crandall stepped away. "I'm through with this witness. For now."

"Strike the question from the record. The jury will disregard it. Would you care to, er, redirect, Mr. Scout?" Blair seemed uncertain.

"No, Your Honor."

"Then you may step down and summon your next . . . witness."

Bartholomew had the next volume ready when his partner returned to their table. His expression told Scout that everything was under control. Scout replied with a grimace that said he hoped he was right.

CHAPTER 9

"The book's title is *My Life on the Plains*. Its author is George Armstrong Custer." Relishing the visible effect of the exalted name upon the jury, the prosecutor reclaimed the slim volume from the judge and strode over to the defense table to show it to Crandall, who fluttered the pages perfunctorily and handed it back.

"I have no objections other than those already raised," he said casually.

The judge glared at him. "Is that an objection, counselor?"

"No, Your Honor."

"Don't keep me guessing. The clerk will label it as evidence."

"In case there is one in this room who is not familiar with the author's name," said Scout, when the book was returned, "he is that same Lieutenant Colonel Custer who lost his life heroically at the Little Big Horn massacre in June of this year, along with every member of his command. This autobiographical account of his experiences as an Indian fighter appeared in a series of articles for *Galaxy* magazine in 1872 and was published in book form two years ago. This is what he wrote about James Butler Hickok, who served him as chief of scouts during the punitive expedition of 1867:

" 'Of his courage there could be no question; it had been brought to the test on too many occasions to admit of a doubt. His skill in the use of the rifle and pistol was unerring; while his deportment was exactly the opposite of what might be expected from a man of his surroundings. It was entirely free from all bluster or bravado. He seldom spoke of himself unless requested to do so. His conversation, strange to say, never bordered either on the vulgar or the blasphemous.' "

He inserted a marker and closed the book, milking the silence that greeted the brief reading; then, with elaborate courtesy, he stepped over to the defense table and presented it to Crandall. The General accepted it in kind, with a smile and a short bow of his head. Rising, he retained the smile.

"Let us hope that the author was a better judge of character than he was of Indians," he commented quietly.

There was a loud guffaw from the rear of the room. Blair jerked upright behind the bench. "Bailiff, remove that man!" A blue vein Scout had not noticed previously throbbed on the judge's right temple. "As for you, General, I warned you what to expect the next time you indulged in these confounded asides. You're in contempt. You will remain where you are until the bailiff has disposed of your unmannerly counterpart in the back row, after which he will escort you to a cell where you will spend the night. Perhaps by morning you will have learned the importance of decorum in a court of law."

The ruling was delivered over miscellaneous grunts and scuffles as the gallery offender, a bearded frontiersman in frayed buckskins, was hoisted to his feet by an arm twisted behind his back and marched out the double doors, all with a minimum of movement on the part of the older and smaller officer. He returned a few moments later for Crandall.

"Damn!" hissed Scout, as the General, looking properly cowed but with a glitter of triumph in his eyes, allowed the bailiff to take his arm.

"I will accept my punishment, Your Honor," he said. "In the meantime I request a recess."

"Granted. Court is adjourned until tomorrow morning at nine."

"The bastard planned it!" His pipe unlighted and forgotten between his teeth, the prosecutor watched a ferry unloading below the office window without seeing it. "For once we caught him off guard, but he bought time as if he had it set aside just for him. What do you want to bet Gannon's with him in his cell right now, planning their next move?"

"No bet," said Bartholomew, ensconced in the leather armchair with *My Life on the Plains* open in his hands. He seemed more interested in the book than in their predicament.

"He plays Blair like a piano."

"Don't sell the judge short. He couldn't very well go on warning Crandall without backing it up. Once the bench relinquishes its control, justice becomes bedlam."

"Put it in Latin and carve it on a portal at Harvard. I've had enough of your wise old sayings for one trial." Scout's tone was bitter.

"Sorry."

He turned from the window. "Don't go hurt on me, Tessie. You know how I am when things aren't going perfectly. But, damn it, we had him on the run! Blair could have fined him or postponed his sentence until the trial was over."

"He lost his temper. Judges have been known to do that on occasion, as have prosecuting attorneys."

"I deserved that. I'm sorry for what I said in the courtroom. I was under pressure."

"But you meant it when you said it." Bartholomew closed the book and looked up at him. "Julian, if you think I'm pushing you too hard, I wish you'd tell me. It's just that staying where you are would be a criminal waste of talent."

"That's where we differ. Grace likes me where I am."

"I thought you didn't want to bring her into it."

"I don't." It came out more abruptly than Scout had intended. Rather than apologize again he decided to drop the topic. "What now?"

"Now, we eat lunch." Bartholomew, who had been consulting his watch, laid aside Custer's book and stood.

"Lunch? Now?"

"It is precisely noon, the usual hour. Let it go, Julian. Our case is set; the burden's on their shoulders, not ours."

"I can't help wondering what they're up to."

"That's healthy." The older attorney took down his coat and tossed the other to his partner. "On our way out, ask your bodyguard where he wants to eat."

After their meal, they repaired to Cody's hotel, where they found the great scout in his room sitting down to an opulent spread surrounded by dazzling silver, a pale-faced waiter lifting the covers off the various dishes for the diner's approval. As he rose to greet his visitors, Bartholomew noted with satisfaction that Cody had exchanged his outlandish frontier garb for a ruffled white shirt and black suit with frock coat. But the famous physique was well in evidence.

"Would you gentlemen care to join me?" he asked, after introductions had been made and hands shaken. "As usual I've ordered considerably more than I require, a habit I fear will ruin me." He patted his stomach and the faint beginnings of a paunch.

The attorneys declined, but accepted seats in a pair of red plush armchairs of a design Buffalo Bill referred to, with unexpected candor, as "whorehouse modern" while he loaded his plate with roast duck and swordfish and mashed potatoes with dark gravy and half a dozen vegetables Scout swore were out of season, and allowed the waiter to fill his glass with white wine. As the hotel employee was leaving, Cody glimpsed the deputy marshal stationed outside the door and asked about him.

"A formality," Scout lied. "The government insists upon overprotecting the prosecution team whenever a celebrated case is being tried. It's a waste of taxpayers' money, but we have nothing to say about it."

"Must be a new policy." Cody chewed thoughtfully. "I'll have to ask General Grant about it the next time I dine at the White House."

Bartholomew changed the subject by explaining that they wished to go over Cody's testimony, which they had decided would take place tomorrow morning in spite of the delay engineered by Crandall. The three spent the next half hour discussing Buffalo Bill's relationship with Hickok while the host demolished the huge meal.

"Wild Bill wasn't cut out for the stage," he announced, refilling his glass for the third time. "I only saw him once more after he left the company in Rochester, when I was camped with the 5th Cavalry on Sage Creek in eastern Wyoming and he got off his train at a ranch nearby. We had a hand or two of poker, but he was on his way to the Black Hills and couldn't tarry. That was in July. After he left we got word of Custer's massacre and were ordered north to join General Crook. It wasn't until I got back East that someone told me Wild Bill had been killed a month after we parted."

"What is your opinion of Hickok's character?" asked Scout. Throughout the narrative he had been making notes in a pad drawn from his breast pocket.

Cody replaced the glass stopper atop the decanter of wine. His hand was steady. Bartholomew caught himself wondering how many glassfuls he could ingest before it wasn't. The frontiersman looked grim.

"I would have trusted him with my life," he said. "Did, in fact, upon more than one occasion."

Smiling, the prosecutor flipped the pad shut. "That's all we need, Colonel. Thank you."

After they had sat politely through the story of the Rawhide Creek battle, which had by then assumed the proportions of a major action, the attorneys thanked their host again and left.

"We've got Crandall by the short hairs now," Scout told Bartholomew, as the lanky deputy fell into step behind them.

"The trial's not over yet," cautioned his partner.

A matinee was playing at the theater that afternoon. Scout obtained tickets and sent a messenger to Grace's home, armed with flowers and an apology for last night, to find out if she cared to accompany him. She did, and at two o'clock he came to collect her. Mrs. Hope was nowhere in sight, for which he was thankful. He asked about her.

"She's locked in her room with her precious newspapers," said Grace, with a gaiety that seemed forced. She had on a bright yellow dress and was tucking her hair beneath a matching bonnet, to the prosecutor's mind a welcome contrast to the bleakness outside. "Have you seen today's?" She handed him the *Daily Press and Dakotaian.* The lead column carried a fairly straightforward account of the trial's first day, but Scout's eyes were drawn to an item near the bottom of the second column.

Correspondence received from a Mr. M. A. Connors, self-confessed *confidant* of Texas outlaw John Wesley Hardin, relates a "set-to" between Hardin and Wild Bill, whose killer is now undergoing trial in Yankton, in which the former, clad only in "long-handles" after dispatching a would-be assassin in Abilene where Wild Bill was marshal, was forced to depart through his hotel room window when the lawman was seen approaching. Reported Hardin to Connors: "Now, Wild Bill had befriended me, but I believed that if he found me in a defenseless condition, he would take no explanation, but would kill me to add to his reputation." The desperado was out of ammunition at the time.

He returned the journal to Grace with a smile and a shake of his head. "They're really on the defendant's side in this one." He helped her on with her wrap, a long one of maroon velvet that went with the rest of her outfit less alarmingly than he might have predicted.

"Doesn't it anger you?" she asked.

"There's no reason it should. The jury is sequestered; they won't see a newspaper or talk to anyone not connected with the court until after the trial."

"Well, it infuriates me. How can a responsible publication side with a murderer?"

"He isn't a murderer until the law proves him one."

"Oh, Julian, don't you ever get upset about anything? Do you never lose your temper?" Patches of color showed through the powder on her cheeks.

Remembering the deputy waiting outside, he took her gently by the elbow and escorted her away from the door. "Something's bothering you besides the paper. What is it?"

Close up, her features were drawn. For the first time since he had known her, she looked like a woman over thirty. "It's Mother. She's getting worse."

He started to say, "Worse than what?" but the agony in her expression stopped him. "Is she ill?"

"No. I mean, yes. But not in the way you think. It's so hard to explain; I don't understand it myself."

He made her sit on the sofa and sank down beside her. The colored maid came in, but withdrew at a signal from him. "You're going to have to start from the beginning, Grace," he said. "My impression has always been that your mother is a very strong woman."

"That's what everyone thinks. It's a pose." She drew a deep breath and told him everything, of how it had been her mother who had found Edgar dead, of her bizarre behavior afterward, of her voracious interest in violence except when it came close to home, of her interview with the doctor and what he had said. The story took less time to tell than she would have believed possible.

"Now she's taken a different turn," Grace went on. "This morning at breakfast she announced that she had seen a strange man watching the house last night from across the street. I thought she might have spotted that deputy you had with you. I told her about him, though I knew she'd be furious with me for keeping it a secret. But the description she gave me didn't sound anything like him." A sudden thought flashed across her features. "Julian, you didn't ask the marshal to post someone here, did you?"

"If I had, I would have told you."

She closed her eyes. She looked drained. "Then it's what I was afraid of. She's having visions."

"What did she say she saw?"

Something in his tone made Grace open her eyes. Julian looked tense. She hesitated. "She said she was watching the street from her window, with the light off. She was in the habit of doing that, she said. I hadn't known that. She claimed she saw a movement in the shadow of a doorway, and then a few minutes later this man came out into the light of the street lamp, glanced up and down the street, then walked away heading west. Do you think she might really have seen something?"

He got up. His expression was unchanged. "I think we should speak with her."

CHAPTER 10

Alone in the parlor with Julian Scout, Marshal Burdick drummed his fingers on his belt buckle and pretended interest in a photograph in an oval frame on the mantel, which depicted a severe-looking old goat with deepset eyes and a grizzled tangle of beard that reached to the second button of his vest. The officer had been in a stormy mood when he arrived, and it had been no help to learn that the man in the picture, who looked to be about Burdick's age, was the father of that comely woman he had coveted from the moment of their introduction. He didn't like to be reminded that he was getting on.

"Mrs. Hope should be down shortly," commented Scout, in an evident attempt at conversation. Burdick ignored it. Lawyers were one more thing for which he had no use.

A large man who had been a bare-knuckles prizefighter in his youth, the marshal had entered law enforcement in 1849 when he became a St. Louis police officer, and but for a few side trips along the way as teamster and boat-hauler and bodyguard he had not left it since. In all that time he had never killed anyone, which he supposed counted for something. Fifty now, graying of hair and moustache, he had been a United States marshal for sixteen months, a position he had sought in the belief that it would enable him to rest while his deputies worked. He deeply resented calls like this one. Hysterical old ladies held little attraction for him.

"I didn't thank you properly for the other night," Scout told him. "Having Grace with me placed me in an awkward situation. We're both grateful."

Burdick glared at him. Well, he sounded sincere. "Forget it. I been rousting drunks since before I could talk."

"Just the same." The prosecutor fidgeted uncomfortably. He had trouble relating to men like Burdick. Ostensibly they were both on the same side, but those who invoked the law and those who enforced it were two entirely different types. "I'm sorry to have to bring you out on this, but some things Mrs. Hope said worried me. If there's anything behind that threat I received, the ones who sent it wouldn't hesitate to try to get to me through Grace."

The marshal said nothing. He had known that assigning that deputy to Scout wouldn't be the end of it. When the officer had come to fetch him half an hour earlier he hadn't been surprised.

After a minute or so of excruciating silence, Mrs. Sargent returned accompanied by a handsome woman of about Burdick's age in a dark gown, whose composed features and firm, manlike grip when he accepted her hand were anything but what he had been expecting. Greetings were followed by an invitation to sit down, after which the maid appeared as if she had been conjured, to offer refreshment. The marshal declined, and she withdrew.

"What did this man you saw look like, Mrs. Hope?" asked Burdick.

Seated across from him in a taffeta-upholstered armchair, she met his gaze steadily, without embarrassment. He marveled at the absence of lines in her face and neck, while the faint creases at the corners of her eyes appealed to him. "I saw him quite clearly when he stepped beneath the street lamp," she said. "He wore a moustache like yours, only his was poorly kept and drooped at the corners. His face was round and his eyes were tiny; they were little more than slits. He had on a derby and a long, shabby overcoat that came down below his knees. His posture was slightly stooped and he walked with a kind of shamble, as if he was more accustomed to riding."

"Did you notice what kind of boots he had on?"

"No. Is that important?"

"Not at all. But if you'd had an answer I would have suspected your story. No one sees everything. What makes you think he was watching this house?"

"I just assumed it. It's the only building directly opposite the doorway he was standing in. If he's been watching any of the others on this side, it doesn't seem as if he'd choose that spot."

"He might have been inside and you just saw him leaving."

She shook her head. "I glimpsed movement in the doorway some minutes earlier. And he was acting suspiciously when he came out, looking everywhere but in this direction. Marshal, are you trying to rattle me?"

"Yes, ma'am."

Scout said, "Do you think she made all this up?" He sounded accusing.

Burdick sat back on the sofa, pursing his lips until he could see his moustache bristling past his nose. "No," he said, at length. "No, I don't. And I don't think she was just seeing things either. I think she saw someone watching this house."

"Mother, please forgive me," Grace said. The older woman placed her hand over her daughter's.

"There's one more question I have to ask." The marshal was embarrassed. He kept his eyes on the floor before the women's feet. "Were either of you ladies, er, disrobing at the time he was across the street?"

"Certainly not!" rapped Mrs. Hope indignantly.

"I was."

Everyone looked at Grace. Her composure was steady, although Scout noticed a faint blush spreading behind her powder. Burdick turned deep red and glanced away.

"Grace!" exclaimed her mother.

She shrugged self-consciously. "My mind was on other things. I'm afraid I wasn't as careful as I usually am. If Mother is right about the time, he was there while I was undressing for bed. Is that what you think he was, Marshal? A Peeping Tom?"

"It would explain it." He picked at the brocade on the arm of his chair. "Then again, it might be coincidence."

"Could this have anything to do with that fellow in the restaurant?" inquired the prosecutor. He too had colored, either from chagrin or from jealousy.

"I doubt it. He was just a drunk. But I'll check it out. In the meantime I'll assign someone to watch the place." He got up. He needed a smoke and there was too much femaleness here. "You folks did the right thing by calling for me. I'm sure it's nothing more than a peeper or someone trying to scare you, like with that note. But it's best to be safe."

"What note is that, Marshal?" Grace was looking at Scout, who seemed uncomfortable. Burdick figured it out.

"Did I speak out of turn?"

"It's all right." The prosecutor took her hands in his. "The other day I got what amounts to a threatening note telling me to drop the McCall case. I'm sure there's nothing to it, but I didn't want to worry you."

"You just went out and got yourself a bodyguard." Her voice was cold.

"I told you, that was Tessie's idea. He can be an old hen sometimes."

"We'll talk about this later, Julian."

"Would you care to share a cigar with me out on the veranda, Mr. Scout?" The marshal accepted his hat and overcoat from the clairvoyant maid.

"We'll talk," echoed the prosecutor, rising.

Outside, Burdick drew a long cigar from an inside pocket and offered it to Scout, who shook his head, holding up his pipe. The marshal shrugged and struck a match on the seat of his pants. "Colder'n a dog's nose," he observed, lips popping on the cigar. "Dry, though, today. It don't get into my bones when it's like this."

"You didn't ask me out here to discuss the weather, Marshal."

"I forgot you was a lawyer." It didn't sound like a compliment. "I didn't want to alarm the womenfolks, but if I was you I'd send them both packing tomorrow."

"You think there's something to these threats?"

"They tried to scare you twice. There ain't any percentage in trying it again. Next time it might be for real."

"We might not even be talking about the same people."

"That's worse. Odds are one of them's playing for keeps. One thing's sure, this wasn't just a Peeping Tom. That's *too* much coincidence."

"I doubt I could persuade them to leave. Not with Grace angry at me."

"That ain't nothing. I was married twenty years and I can tell you that the woman ain't been born that could hold a good mad. She'll come around."

"I'll try. But Mrs. Hope is dead set on staying until the mansion is sold."

"She's nervy, I'll give her that much." Burdick buttoned his overcoat. "That won't dump no scales in her favor when she's looking down the wrong end of a six-shooter. Don't they pay you lawyer fellows to argue?"

"I gather you don't favor the profession."

"It ain't the profession, it's them that follow it. Out here, before it got safe enough to bring you fellows out with your briefcases and habeus corpuses and slick talk, we used to hang killers and horse thieves. Now we ask them would they please kindly say they done something not as bad as what we know they done so's we can lock them up for a spell and get on to the next killer or horse thief."

"You have to admit the machinery needed oil, Marshal."

"I miss the squeak."

They smoked for a while in silence. Then Scout said, "You mentioned a wife. Where is she now?"

"She's dead."

"I'm sorry."

"It wasn't you done it. It was the smallpox." There were two inches of ash on the end of the cigar. He reached up and tapped it off with the end of a blunt forefinger. "I read where this Johnny Varnes was mixed up in the plot to kill Wild Bill."

"That's what McCall claimed before he changed his story again. He said Varnes paid him to do it."

"That could be where he got the gold dust to play poker with the day before. I read about that in today's paper."

"Possibly. Why?"

Burdick shrugged a bearlike shoulder. "Nothing much. Just that I know this Varnes by reputation. He's meaner'n a gunny sack full of bees. I'd hate to think he was in on what we got here. Well, I'll send someone around to keep an eye on the place." He stepped off the porch and left after exchanging a few words with Scout's bodyguard, slouched against the nearby street lamp. The prosecutor was still standing there minutes after his pipe went out.

General Crandall had the cell nearest the stove on the ground floor of the city jail. Orville Gannon, accompanied by the guard, found him seated on the cot reading the *Daily Press and Dakotaian* and chuckling. He glanced up when the key rattled in the lock.

"This piece on John Wesley Hardin has got to be Magruder's. It's his style down to the ground. Have you seen it?" He folded the paper to the second column and handed it to his partner as he stepped inside. The guard clanged shut the door, muttered something about fifteen minutes, and left, his hobnail boots clip-clopping on the oaken floorboards.

"Free people have to buy their own newspapers," Gannon replied, glancing at the two-inch item. He handed the paper back. "Isn't Magruder the one who did the restaurant story?"

Crandall nodded, eyeing him closely. He looked less jovial without his necktie, which he had surrendered at the time of his incarceration, along with his suspenders and beloved watch and chain. "You don't approve, do you?"

The gaunt man's expression was unreadable. "You have your methods and I have mine. I just happen to believe that cases can be won or lost from the books without recourse to chicanery."

"If I believed that, I'd retire tomorrow. How does it look?"

"Not good. All this quibbling about Hickok's character is hurting us. The better they make him look, the worse McCall comes off. If we don't return to the specifics of the case, he'll swing."

"The hell with that. The specifics of the case is McCall killed Hickok in cold blood. Did you bring the stuff?"

Gannon opened his briefcase and drew out the thick sheaf of books and dusty clippings, tied loosely with a cord. "The turnkey spent ten minutes making sure I didn't have a derringer hidden among the pages." He deposited it on the bunk beside Crandall.

The prisoner untied the cord. "If we can introduce half of this stuff into evidence, McCall will not only walk out of that courtroom a free man, Blair'll lend him a hundred dollars out of his own pocket to give him a fresh start."

"I didn't realize you took such an interest in your client's future."

"I don't. He's physically incapable of telling the truth, and every time I confer with him I make sure to leave my wallet at home first. Besides, he's crazy."

"Then why defend him?"

Crandall looked up at his partner in surprise. "You're a lawyer—figure it out."

"Let it go, John. I'm not some green Harvard graduate you can take in with that speech about the Constitution. You've a personal stake in this somewhere."

"I want Bartholomew's scalp." The portly attorney lay the clipping he had been reading in his lap. "When I heard Scout was prosecuting I pulled every political string I knew to get the appointment as public defender, because Scout doesn't sneeze but that Bartholomew is right there with a handkerchief. You wouldn't know it, being a book lawyer"—the condescension in his tone stirred Gannon's atrophied emotions—"but that cornpone-eater has a reputation in the legal profession equal to Hickok's among assassins. I want it."

"He doesn't have it anymore. I beat him in that assault case."

"I've seen the transcripts. He never had a chance. The judge and jury were Yankees and his drawl makes General Lee sound like a Canadian. He won it on appeal and a change of venue."

"I didn't prosecute in appellate."

"Just as well. He'd have picked you cleaner than a dowager's false teeth."

Gannon ignored the slight. His complexion looked grayer than usual in the minimal illumination filtering through the cell window. "So you win, and his reputation is yours. What then?"

"Politics, perhaps. I'm told I'd make a fine senator. But at this point that hardly concerns me. Bartholomew's scalp will be ample enough reward."

"What about Scout?"

"He's sharper than I thought. But he's tactics and Tessie is strategy. Remove the general and you take out the company commander."

"If McCall is crazy, why don't you plead insanity?"

"That would be cheating."

"It's your case." Carefully arranging the crease in his trousers, the gaunt man sat on the other end of the cot. "Cody testifies tomorrow."

Crandall looked at him sharply. "How do you know?"

He allowed himself a faint smile. There was no warmth in it. "You aren't the only one with convenient friends. The deputy marshal guarding Scout owes me a favor. He was outside Cody's hotel room when they went over his testimony."

"He didn't hear what they said?"

"I didn't ask and he didn't say. Those are grounds for disbarment in every state and territory in the Union. But the odds are they'll put him on the stand in the morning."

"I suppose that's what we get for waiving our right to interview all character witnesses before the trial. Well, there's plenty of stuff here on Cody and Hickok." He thumbed through the material. "I don't suppose you've talked McCall out of testifying."

"I tried. He's dead set on it, to the point of firing us if we refuse to let him."

"We'll just have to make the best of it," said Crandall. "How's our witness?"

"Cheerful. Are you sure you want to put him on? McCall's bad enough, but I shudder to think what Scout will do with this one's past."

"Let me worry about that."

"I never worry."

I believe it, thought the other. Aloud he said, "You mentioned that Scout's still being guarded. There haven't been any more threats on his life?"

"Only if his lady friend's mother is to be believed. She claims she saw someone watching the house last night."

"Son of a bitch!" Crandall smote the stack of documents with a pudgy palm. A gray cloud billowed out around it. The guard came clattering down the corridor at the report. Gannon explained and he withdrew reluctantly.

"Forget about it," said Gannon. "The jury's sequestered. There's no way the news can reach them."

"It's not the jury that worries me. It's Blair." The General had calmed somewhat, though his face was still cherry-red. "If he gets wind of it, he could say the threats were affecting Scout's judgment and declare a mistrial."

"So what? It would buy time."

"I'm not interested in that kind of time. Scout wouldn't be assigned to a second trial and I'd be facing someone besides Bartholomew. I don't want to win that way."

"I don't think your client would agree."

Crandall displayed his eyeteeth. "Nobility fits you like a tent. The only reason you agreed to go partners with me on this one was to reacquaint yourself with courtroom tactics."

Gannon stood. The guard had returned, his watch clutched significantly in one hand. "Remind me not to work with you again."

His partner remained seated. His expression was grim again. "Hire me a Pinkerton. I want the one who's been making those threats put out of the way. I don't care how it's done."

"You've got it," said Gannon, and left, unaware of the half-dozen pairs of ears that had been listening and the one pair of lips that would repeat the conversation outside the stone walls of the building.

CHAPTER 11

"State your full name and occupation, please."

"William Frederick Cody, scout and lecturer."

The flashpan of a camera Judge Blair had reluctantly allowed to be set up in the aisle erupted in a blinding, blue-white flame that drew a collective gasp from the gallery and a start from the bench, preserving for posterity the tableau of the great frontiersman being interrogated by Julian Scout. Cody was unaffected; with Hickok dead he bade fair toward becoming the most photographed man of the nineteenth century. Today Buffalo Bill was turned out modestly but well in a black Prince Albert and striped trousers tucked into the high tops of boots that shone blue. Bartholomew, seated at the prosecution table, had cursed when the people's star witness unbuttoned his coat to sit and exhibited the gaudiest belt buckle the attorney had ever seen, fashioned from silver with a diamond-studded buffalo head in the center, the entire thing the size of a hotel ashtray. But he had to smile when Cody caught his eye and favored him with a very solemn wink. He was a hard man to stay mad at.

"You are the same William Frederick Cody who defeated the Cheyenne chief Yellow Hand at Rawhide Creek in eastern Wyoming Territory last July?"

"Objection," said Crandall at the defense table, looking little the worse for his night in jail. "Irrelevant."

"Your Honor, I am merely seeking to establish the witness' credibility by bringing his heroic career to light," Scout protested.

"I think we are all familiar with the details of Mr. Cody's estimable life on the prairie, counselor. Sustained."

The witness inclined his head cordially in response to Blair's compliment. Scout continued.

"When did you meet James Butler Hickok?"

"The year was 1861," said Cody. "I was living with my mother and five sisters near Leavenworth, Kansas. My father had died four years before, and at fifteen I was the sole support of my family. Jim —that was the name by which Hickok was known at that time— came to Leavenworth that year as an army wagon boss out of Sedalia, Missouri. I hired on as his assistant."

"How would you describe the association?"

"Amiable," said Cody, and laughed. It was infectious. Bartholomew felt the spectators warming to him. "Jim had with him a fast-running horse from the mountains that he thought could beat anything on four legs. Well, I have always been a good rider, and in those days I was a good deal smaller than I am now. While sharing a flask over the campfire one night he proposed a partnership. He was to enter the horse in the St. Louis races with me riding. We would bet every cent we had, including the horse." He paused, lost in the memory.

"And?" Scout prompted.

He laughed again. "Well, the long and the short of it is we came out of that race minus the horse and everything we owned in the world—dead busted in the largest city we had ever been in. It seems the horse was not as swift on the flats as it had been in the mountains."

Laughter rippled through the gallery. Amused himself, Blair let it go.

Scout smiled in appreciation of the humor. "What did Hickok do then?"

"He did something that was characteristic of his generous nature. He borrowed money to buy me a steamboat ticket back home."

"But that was not the last you saw of each other."

"By no means." Cody sat back, folding his rather small hands across his stomach in the attitude he seemed to love best, that of storyteller. "Shortly after my return to Leavenworth I joined up with the 7th Kansas Volunteer Cavalry as scout with the rank of private. In the fall of 1864 I donned civilian clothes and rode ahead along the Little Blue River near Independence, Missouri, to gather information concerning the disposition of Rebel troops. Stopping to water my horse at a farmhouse, I was invited to step inside for a bite, where I discovered a man in the garb of a Confederate officer seated at a table.

"Now, I had succeeded in putting past the locals my pose as a drifter, but the sight of a professional soldier—the enemy, as it were, in all his array—caused me no little apprehension. I was grateful for my side arm, and was prepared to make use of it should my story fail to convince, when he turned about in his seat, studied me for a moment, and said, 'You little rascal, what are you doing in those secessionist clothes?' It was Jim Hickok, disguised as a Rebel to perform much the same function as I was myself."

This time the judge was obliged to quell the mirth with his gavel. As it died, Crandall raised a hand, smiling.

"I must confess, Your Honor, that while I find Colonel Cody's anecdotes amusing, I fail to see how they bear upon the case at hand."

"You don't?" The judge looked surprised. "Mr. Scout's line of questioning seems fairly straightforward to me. However, we'll let him explain. Mr. Scout?"

The prosecutor nodded. "Your Honor, a friendship is an intricate thing, developed over a long period of time and built of numerous incidents that seem meaningless when they occur but that in the aggregate are of importance to the whole. The state intends to establish the credibility of the witness' character references by exploring the depths of his relationship with the deceased."

"Well put, counselor, though you might have been more succinct. Objection overruled."

"Exception," said Crandall. "I didn't understand one word Mr. Scout said."

Bellowing laughter rocked the courtroom. Blair banged his gavel for two minutes until it subsided. The vein appeared on his forehead.

"May I remind you people," he said gravely, "that a man is on trial here for his life."

The announcement had a sobering effect upon the spectators. But for miscellaneous coughs and scuffles it was quiet in the room. Scout broke the spell.

"To your knowledge, Colonel Cody, how did James Butler Hickok acquire the nickname 'Wild Bill'?"

The frontiersman looked grave. Blair's admonition had had its effect upon him as well. "As I understand it, it was given him during a fracas in Independence shortly after we parted company the first time. There was a riot in a saloon, and he came to the bartender's aid. When the mob was preparing to rush the establishment, Jim fired two shots over their heads and said, 'If you folks don't clear the street I'll shoot the next man that moves toward me.' The gang broke up. Later that night, a woman spotted him at a vigilance committee meeting and shouted, 'Good for you, Wild Bill!' Something to that effect. The name stuck."

This was pure hearsay, and Blair looked to the defense table to see if Crandall was going to raise an objection. But the General seemed intent on perforating a typewritten sheet of paper with his pencil. The holes formed the outline of a shapely female form.

"Tell us about the next time you and Hickok met," prodded the prosecutor.

"The war had been over for more than a year. I was married by then, had acquired and sold a hotel in Salt Creek Valley, Kansas, and returned to the freedom of the plains. We were reunited in Junction City, where Jim—Wild Bill, now—was working for the army as a civilian scout out of Fort Riley. He was an impressive figure in those days, I can tell you—over six feet, lean as a puma, fine-featured, long of lock and swaggering of stride in buckskin leggings and red shirt and broad-brimmed hat, with two pistols in his belt and a rifle in his hand. Recruits and officers alike wrote home about him. Once again he rescued me from unemployment by getting me assigned as one of his fellows. I spent the next year in that capacity, carrying dispatches and guiding expeditions through Indian territory. This was my first job as a civilian scout, and I can hardly say that it has not worked to my advantage."

"Was it Hickok who nicknamed you Buffalo Bill?"

Cody chuckled. "No, and I wish I could say that it was bestowed upon me in gratitude for supplying Union Pacific track layers with buffalo meat. The fact of it is that it sprang from a ditty composed by a laborer who had grown heartily sick of the same fare day in and day out. It went something like this." He cleared his throat and began singing, in an unexpectedly clear tenor:

> "Buffalo Bill, Buffalo Bill,
> Never missed and never will;
> Always aims and shoots to kill
> And the company pays his buffalo bill."

The story and scrap of doggerel was appreciated by the spectators, among whom there was a smattering of applause. Blair rapped his gavel sharply to remind them of his late rebuke.

"Did you save Hickok's life on more than one occasion?" Scout queried.

"I was nothing more than an instrument," corrected the witness modestly. "I was scouting with General Eugene A. Carr's 5th Cavalry during the winter of 1868 in Colorado Territory when word reached us that Brigadier General William Penrose, with four companies of the 10th Cavalry and one of the 7th, was stranded by snowstorms on Palo Duro Creek on the border of Texas and the Nations. Wild Bill had been guiding them. We left Fort Lyon in December with a pack train of emergency supplies.

"It was a terrible winter. The temperature was thirty below and drifts were piled as high as fifteen feet. Scouting ahead with a small party, I came upon one of Penrose's old camps and traced his trail along the Cimarron River while Carr followed along the opposite bank with the wagons. We were in the Raton foothills when Carr stopped, uncertain that he could get the wagons down a steep slope to the river. I crossed over and talked him into getting his cavalry down, then turned to the wagonmasters and told them to run down, slide down or fall down, as long as they got down. When still they hesitated, I fetched a mess wagon to the edge of the slope, had all four wheels locked in place with chains, and started down. The mules went along slowly and well until we got near the bottom, when they panicked and broke into a gallop, not stopping until we rattled smack dab into the middle of General Carr's cavalry. The other wagons followed suit, and in half an hour we were all in camp.

"Shortly thereafter, still following Penrose's trail, we came upon three half-dead troopers whose narrative of their outfit's ordeal prompted Carr to order me ahead with two cavalry companies and a fifty-mule pack train of supplies. Thus equipped, I pulled into Penrose's camp some days later, where I found my old friend Wild Bill hunkered over a small fire thawing out his shooting hand. I don't believe that we were any too soon, for he and his comrades had begun to slaughter their horses for meat."

A spellbinder of many years' experience, Cody paused to let his listeners absorb what he had said before continuing. Wood crackling in the stove was the loudest sound in the room.

"I didn't see Wild Bill again until early the following year, when he was brought into Fort Lyon three-quarters dead and bleeding copiously from an ugly wound in the thigh. I learned that he had fallen into a running fight with a band of Cheyennes while riding alone across the prairie and caught a lance high and deep. He was found about a mile from the fort by a firewood detail the next morning. When I saw him I took charge and rushed him to the surgeon. He recovered, but the wound ended his career as a scout. He was just thirty-one, one year older than I am now."

"But that was not the end of your association."

"There is one more episode to relate, though I must admit that it is not very heroic. In 1873 I allowed my friend Ned Buntline to talk me into appearing in his stage drama, *Scouts of the Prairie,* on its eastern tour. Wild Bill had by this time gained considerable fame, having been written about in *Harper's New Monthly* and the *Weekly Missouri Democrat,* and featured in DeWitt's Ten Cent Romances. I wired him from New York City to come join me." He shook his head, smiling. "It was a disaster. He did not take to show business and demonstrated his dislike for it at every opportunity. I suppose it was because he was so accustomed to the real thing that he could not bring himself to take acting seriously. He left the show in Rochester and went back West. That was the last time I saw him, but for a brief meeting in Wyoming last July, shortly before he was murdered."

"Objection!" barked Crandall.

"Sustained. The witness will confine his remarks to those things he knows as fact."

Scout took advantage of the exchange to sneak a look at McCall. The defendant had ceased staring at the floor and was concentrating on the eagle atop the staff of the American flag behind Blair's left shoulder. His expression was as sullen as ever. The prosecutor returned his attention to Cody.

"Did you consider Hickok a replacement for your father?"

The witness frowned, either deep in thought or wishing to appear so. He seemed never to forget his place at the center of things, particularly where the women in the courtroom were concerned. Scout had seen a dreamy look in more than one pair of feminine eyes as Cody was being sworn in, and had noted reciprocation on the part of the great frontiersman.

"I did not look upon him as such," he said at length, "though there was nine years' difference in our ages, and it might be said that his interest in me was paternal. No, our friendship was just that, a friendship. But I'll never know another one as sweet."

"How would you sum up your friend's character?"

Cody might have been anticipating the question, for he answered without pausing.

"When the Indian menace is settled, law and order established throughout the land, and men are free to lay aside their arms in favor of more constructive pursuits, Wild Bill will stand unique as a man long after the necessity for his existence is extinguished. While probably no other in western history had so many notches on his gun, it may be said that no other recorded them oftener in defending right. I am proud to have known him."

Scout heard scribbling and lamented that when the witness' words appeared in print they would sound false and self-serving. No one who had not been present when they were expressed could realize the depth of sincerity behind them. The prosecutor wished the trial were over at this moment. But it wasn't close; the end wasn't even in sight. He turned away with a sigh.

"Your witness, General."

CHAPTER 12

Advancing through a pool of silence, Crandall pulled up a few feet short of the witness box. Cody's strength of will had been demonstrated and he evidently saw no advantage in violating the witness' personal space. Scout reflected that his opponent seemed no more humble for having incurred the judge's displeasure overnight. If anything, there was more bounce in his step than usual.

"First off, Colonel," he said blandly, "allow me to express my appreciation on behalf of the rest of the country for your heroic efforts to render the West a safe place to raise a family. We are all aware—"

"Your Honor," interrupted the prosecutor, "if this is a testimonial dinner, where is my serving?"

Blair fought back the laughter with his gavel. His expression was severe. "Objection sustained. In the future, Mr. Scout, the state will refrain from these childish attempts at whimsy."

Crandall appeared unmoved by the digression. "Colonel, I take it from your mention of the horse-racing episode in St. Louis that the deceased was a gambling man. How did he react to his loss on this occasion?"

"He was philosophical about it. I would not go so far as to say that he was not disappointed, but he had won and lost enough times to accept the caprices of fate."

"Did you gamble with him on any other occasion?"

"It is one of the few diversions which life in the open spaces allows."

"Answer the question, please."

"I thought I had. Yes, I gambled with him many times."

"What sort of winner would you say he was?"

"Objection," said Scout. "This entire line of questioning is irrelevant."

Crandall turned to the bench. "I refer Your Honor to Carl

Mann's comments upon Hickok's winning attitude at the poker table in Saloon No. 10."

"Objection overruled," said Blair. "Proceed, General."

"Colonel Cody?"

"I never knew Wild Bill to be anything but humble about his gains," the witness replied.

"I see." The lawyer fiddled with his elk's tooth. "Are you aware of what saloon owner Mann had to say upon the same subject in this court the day before yesterday?"

"I read what the local newspaper reported," said Cody, meeting his gaze. "Not knowing Mr. Mann, I will not call him a liar behind his back."

The gallery hummed. The judge allowed the noise to die out on its own.

Crandall pushed on. "Colonel Cody, you told this court that you joined the Union Army shortly after your return from St. Louis, is that correct?"

"I said that I joined the army. I don't remember saying that it was shortly after my return."

"Oh, but you did. Would you like the recorder to read it?" He raised his eyebrows to the judge, who nodded to the man at the small desk. The recorder went back through his notes.

"That won't be necessary," said Cody. "I concede that I said it. But it was just an expression. It was three years before I joined the regular army."

"Why so long, Colonel?"

"I was underage. My mother would not give her consent, as I was the sole support of my family. I consoled myself by acting as guide for various military and volunteer units."

Crandall strode over to the defense table and returned bearing a scrap of paper. "This article appeared in an eastern newspaper two years ago." He handed it to the judge, who donned his glasses, skimmed the fine print, and gave it back. The General extended the clipping to Cody. "Do you remember making these statements?"

The witness glanced at the item and smiled sheepishly. "I fear I do."

"Shall I read them?"

"That won't be necessary." Cody closed his eyes. "Asked how I spent my time when I was not guiding troops, I replied that for the most part I led a dissolute and reckless life. When I did join the army a few days before my eighteenth birthday, I had no idea of doing anything of the kind, but one day, after having been under the influence of bad whiskey, I awoke to find myself a soldier in the 7th Kansas. I did not remember how or when I had enlisted, but I saw I was in for it, and that it would not do for me to endeavor to back out."

"Thank you, Colonel," said Crandall, when the gallery had calmed down. "Now, which of your statements are we to assume is the truth? The one you made to the journalist who penned this article, or the one you made under oath a few moments ago?"

Cody's face was stony. "Are you calling me a liar, sir?"

Scout closed his eyes and said, "Shit."

"The witness is instructed to answer the question," said Blair.

"Both are true. My mother would not allow me to join, and when I did I was not in full possession of my faculties."

"Very well," said Crandall. "I ask you again: What sort of winner was Hickok?"

Scout shot to his feet. "Objection! The witness has already answered that question. Counsel for the defense is badgering him!"

"Sustained. The question will be stricken and the jury will disregard it."

The General looked serene. He had made his point. "We move on, Colonel. I confess that your account of the valiant rescue of General Penrose's command during the winter of 1868 stirred me. I was disappointed, however, when you failed to finish it. Did you, once you had reached Penrose's camp, accompany, with Hickok, an expedition to join Colonel A. W. Evans' column coming east from New Mexico Territory?"

Cody seemed to know what was coming. Cautiously, he replied in the affirmative.

"And did you, when you were camped on the south fork of the Canadian River, learn that a Mexican wagon train was on its way to Evans' supply depot with a cargo of beer?"

"We did," said the witness, and added hastily, "Before you continue—"

"A simple yes or no will suffice, Colonel. Did you bribe the Mexicans into giving you the beer meant for the men of Evans' command, then return to your own camp with the cargo and sell it by the cup at a profit?"

Cody, his eyes smoldering, said nothing. A buzzing swept through the audience.

"The witness is instructed to answer the question," Blair pointed out.

Crandall didn't wait. Producing the newspaper clipping: "Did you, Colonel Cody, tell the journalist who penned this article, quote, 'The result was one of the biggest beer jollifications I ever had the misfortune to attend'?"

"It was war," blurted the scout. "The winter was hard and spirits were low. The men needed something—"

"—that you and Hickok were more than willing to supply for your own gain," finished Crandall. "We all understand your motives, Colonel."

"Objection!" roared Scout. "Now counsel for the defense is drawing conclusions."

"Sustained. Have you learned nothing from your incarceration, General?"

"I object to the bench upbraiding defense counsel with the jury present."

All eyes swung to the gaunt man who had risen from the defense table. These were the first words Orville Gannon had spoken in the courtroom since the trial had begun. He stood in the center of a shocked silence, as stiff and bland-looking as a well-dressed scarecrow.

"Overruled." It had taken Judge Blair a moment to react.

"Exception," said Gannon.

"Noted. Mr. Gannon, are you and General Crandall taking turns, like relay runners?"

"No, Your Honor."

"Then please sit down. I won't have two attorneys pleading the same case simultaneously."

Gannon sat.

"They're going at him from two sides," whispered Bartholomew. "Keeping him off balance."

Scout, staring at the bench, acted as if he hadn't heard. He was still seething over what the General was doing to his witness, or maybe it was Cody he was mad at. Bartholomew felt sorry for the frontiersman. An amusing anecdote of a wartime prank related for a reporter's edification became something quite different in a court of law. Crandall's instinct for material beneficial to his case was uncanny.

"One more thing, Colonel, and then I'll let you go." The General sounded fatherly. "Tell us about your friend Wild Bill's experiences while a member of your theatrical troupe."

Cody fidgeted, obviously wishing he had stayed in New York. "I spoke of that. He did not take to the profession and returned West before the tour was over."

"It's been written about, Colonel. Shall I read some of the notices?" Crandall took a step toward the defense table, stacked high with papers.

"No," said the witness quickly. Then, inexplicably, he smiled. "No, General, I'd rather these good people heard it from me directly."

He sat back, in control of himself once again. There was a whisper of pages as the journalists in the front row turned to fresh sheets in their pocket pads. "I regretted having made the offer the moment Wild Bill arrived at the Breevort Hotel in New York City and knocked down his driver for charging too much," Cody began. "That was not the end of it by any means. The first time a spotlight was shone upon him he hurled his pistol at it and shattered the glass. On stage during a performance, he spat out the cold tea which served for whiskey and demanded the real thing or he would 'tell no stories,' as he put it. While laying over in Titusville, Pennsylvania, he got into an altercation with a gang of oil-field roughnecks in a saloon and bludgeoned them with a chair. Finally, in Rochester, New York, he commanded a grip to 'tell that long-haired son of a bitch'— meaning myself—'that I have no more use for him or his damned show business,' and deserted. No one was very sorry to find him gone."

The decorum of the courtroom dissolved in mirth. Blair, who had found himself smiling at the account, tried furiously for a few moments to regain control with his gavel and gave up. Scout let go an obscenity, making Bartholomew glad of the noise that drowned it out. When at length the din showed signs of subsiding, the judge employed his gavel again to maintain the illusion that he was on top of things, and asked the prosecutor in a loud voice if he cared to redirect. Scout rose, then seemed to think better of it and sank back down, shaking his head.

"Your Honor, the state rests."

BOOK TWO

THE DEFENSE

Whenever you get into a row, be sure and not shoot too quick.
I've known many a fellow slip up for shooting in a hurry.

—James Butler Hickok, 1865

CHAPTER 13

The stranger's card was a riot of scrollwork dominated by a darkly watchful eye, beneath which was printed "We never sleep" and around which skirled PINKERTON'S NATIONAL DETECTIVE AGENCY in circus letters. The words "Calvin Lucy, Special Operative" were all but crowded off the bottom. Long fingers with clean nails displayed the card at the end of a slim arm in a black sleeve.

The deputy on duty at the Sargent home studied the newcomer, taking in his trim form and long, tanned face with its carefully trimmed Van Dyke beneath a high silk hat that shone softly in the sunlight of late morning. "Got any other identification?"

"Here is my badge and a letter of introduction from the man who engaged me."

The badge, an impressive gold shield, made similar use of the all-seeing eye, and the letter, with the unfamiliar name Orville Gannon scratched across the bottom, looked official. The embossed letterhead read "General J. Q. A. Crandall," a name the deputy did recognize from the paper. But he was still suspicious. Perhaps it was the stranger's slight southern accent; he himself had fought the war on the winning side.

"You don't look like no Pinkerton I ever seen."

"The fact disturbs me more than words can relate." The man identified as Lucy appeared patient. His breath formed vapors in the frosty air of the porch.

"Marshal Burdick said not to let anyone in till he gets back."

The letter was folded and put away with the badge in the other's inside breast pocket. "How much experience have you had protecting your fellow citizens from attack?"

"I've guarded prisoners plenty of times. Anyway, what business is it of yours?"

"It's hardly the same. I'll wager you've had none." His gray eyes swept over the brick front of the jail-like structure. "This is a large building. I imagine it has several entrances. How will you watch them all?"

"There's another man in back." The deputy thrust out a black-bearded jaw. The gesture made him look older, almost thirty.

"I suppose he's stationed outside as well. There should be a man in the house."

"You, I suppose."

The stranger said nothing.

"Just how much do *you* know about protecting folks?"

"I helped spare the President from an assassin's bullet last year."

"Go to hell! I never heard about it."

"You weren't meant to. Will you let me pass, or shall I make contact with your superior? I warn you that every moment of delay increases the danger to the ladies."

The deputy fingered his Winchester and frowned. Decisions bothered him. He much preferred to follow clear orders. Still, the man seemed to know something he didn't, and he hated to think what would happen if he turned him away and something went wrong. Marshaling suited him better than robbing express offices. "I got to frisk you for weapons."

The stranger looked at him pitifully. "Of what earthly use is an unarmed bodyguard?"

"We'll talk about that when the marshal comes. Get 'em up."

Sighing, the man called Lucy lifted his arms while the other patted him down expertly. He didn't stop when he came up with a .38 caliber Remington from a special holster sewn inside the man's vest, but continued all the way down, taking special care with his dyed black calfskin boots, in which a derringer or a knife could be concealed. As an afterthought he removed the silk hat and felt the lining inside. There were no other weapons.

"All right, you can go in." He thrust the confiscated revolver under his belt.

"Don't I get a receipt?"

"I won't sell it while you're inside, if that's what you're worried about," the deputy snapped.

The Pinkerton card got the stranger past the maid and into the parlor, where Grace Sargent met him. Her mother was on the settee with a book open in her lap. She nodded at his greeting.

"Your firm has an honorable reputation," said Grace, after amenities had been exchanged. "However, I feel the authorities are doing an admirable job. Forgive me, but your presence seems superfluous."

He smiled easily. He had surrendered his hat to the maid and the lamplight cast blue halos off his wavy hair. "With all due respect to Marshal Burdick's deputies, ma'am, they are at their best when apprehending felons and preventing their escape. Personal security is a Pinkerton specialty."

"Did Mr. Scout engage your services?"

"Our client is General Crandall, the counsel for the defense in the McCall trial." Noting the expression that crossed the women's faces, he added hastily, "While it may be uncommon for an attorney to arrange for the protection of his opponent's acquaintances, it is not unheard of. The General wishes to avoid prejudicing his case. If you'd prefer, I can send for Mr. Scout."

"Mother?" Grace looked to the older woman on the settee.

"It's your house, dear," said Mrs. Hope coolly.

Her daughter made a decision and nodded. "That won't be necessary, Mr. Lucy. Julian is in court and should not be disturbed. How can we help?"

"Could you gather the household in this room for a few moments? Just so I'll know a strange face should I see one later."

There were five servants, including the housekeeper, two maids, the cook, and a handyman. They arranged themselves in front of the Pinkerton, the cook wiping her large black hands impatiently on her apron. She smelled of baking bread.

"Is this the entire staff?" he asked incredulously.

Grace nodded. "We had a butler, but Mother let him go and engaged Mrs. Hurley as housekeeper in his place. His salary demands were exorbitant."

"Five people can manage a house twice this size," Mrs. Hope explained. "Keeping more servants than one needs is an unholy waste of funds."

"Does any of them own a firearm?"

"No," said Grace, but the handyman, a wizened little Greek with oily black hair and a limp moustache, raised a tentative hand. The Pinkerton riveted on him.

"Is it on the premises?" The Greek nodded. "Please get it."

The handyman withdrew, to return moments later bearing a well-used Colt pocket revolver, .31 caliber, with an octagonal barrel and a stagecoach holdup engraved on the cylinder, worn nearly all the way off. All five chambers were loaded and the caps were in place.

"It will have to do," said the Pinkerton, examining the museum piece. "I must say, the size of the household made me wonder if I'd be even this fortunate. But there's always one to be found." Smiling thinly, he cocked it and pointed the muzzle at the astonished group in front of him. "You will all remain where you are until I instruct you otherwise."

The cook began to whimper. The maids kept silent, but one of them, the white one from upstairs, was quivering uncontrollably. The handyman, evidently blaming himself for this turn of events, looked shamefaced. The housekeeper looked affronted. Dora Hope was pale but composed, grasping her daughter's hand resting on her shoulder. Grace was the first to recover from the shock.

"What happened to the real Calvin Lucy?" she demanded. "It's obvious you're no Pinkerton agent."

"He's been detained until Judgment Day. You will all remain silent." There was now no trace of cordiality in the gunman's tone.

As though enjoying the attention it was getting, the clock on the mantel ticked away the minutes loudly. Even the cook was quiet, though her lips continued to move, mouthing a prayer under her breath. The wind had come up and from time to time a bare branch scrabbled across the windowpanes. Grace lost patience.

"What are we waiting for? Who are you?"

"I won't ask for silence twice." The way he said it, with the antiquated but deadly looking revolver clasped rock-steady in his hand, brought a breath of winter chill into the heated room.

After what seemed an hour, but which when Grace stole a glance at the clock turned out to be no more than fifteen minutes, three knocks sounded clearly from the rear of the house. There was a pause, followed by two more raps.

"Over here, Mrs. Sargent." The bogus detective beckoned with the revolver. "We'll answer it together."

She hesitated. Mrs. Hope tightened her grip on her hand.

"I'll kill someone," he said. "It might as well be your mother."

Grace said, "You won't shoot. It would bring the deputies."

"I am a desperate man, Mrs. Sargent. Do you know me well enough to take that chance?"

She considered it. He shrugged and tightened his finger on the trigger. She patted her mother's hand and came over to him.

"Ladies first," he said, indicating the curtained doorway. To the others, "If anyone opens his mouth or moves from this room I'll blow out her heart."

To Grace, who had not made it in some time, the journey from the parlor to the back door was longer than she remembered. The air in the kitchen was hazy with smoke; instinctively she took a step toward the stove, in the oven of which a loaf of bread was shriveling slowly. The revolver dug into her back. "Let it burn."

She stopped before the door leading outside, awaiting instructions.

"Answer it," he commanded. "Just in case. Think of the person on the other side before you decide to try something." He moved over to the wall.

Unlocking and opening the door, she caught her breath to scream, but was cut off when the false detective's hand was clasped over her mouth from behind.

The man standing on the back porch was thickset and slightly stooped, with a round face and vicious little eyes crowded together just under the brim of his derby. A frayed overcoat badly in need of brushing hung below his knees. The open clasp knife in his left hand glistened red. When he saw the man who had called himself Lucy he relaxed his stance and wiped the blade clean with a yellowed handkerchief.

"Get in here," snarled the man holding Grace. "You look like a maniac."

Not until the man was inside and the door was locked did he release his grip. Grace was left with a faint scent of toilet water in her nostrils from his hand. "Did you have to kill him?" he demanded. He was quivering with rage.

"No, I figured I'd ask him to leave, but he didn't take to the idea." The man's voice was an insinuating whisper. She suspected that this was its normal tone. "Don't worry, I drug him behind a hedge and covered him with snow. They won't find him on their own before the next thaw. You get the other one?"

"You fool, don't you see you've ruined everything?"

"I'm here, ain't I? Listen, Johnny—"

"Shut up, you idiot!" It came out like a lash.

The newcomer remained uncowed. His eyes lit on Grace and lingered, moving her to clasp her throat. She felt as if he could see through her clothes. "This her? Why don't we just grab her and go?"

"The plan was to hold her here. Put away that pig-sticker and give me your pistol."

"Why?" He looked suspicious.

The one called Johnny showed him the revolver he had captured. "You're used to using a cap and ball. I'm not."

His partner pocketed the closed knife and handed him a .44 caliber Smith & Wesson from his belt in return for the old Colt. Then they returned to the parlor, Grace walking in front.

"Keep them covered while I see to the other deputy," said the false Pinkerton.

"You sure you don't want to hire someone else to do it for you?" sneered the other.

His partner looked at him sadly. "You stupid fool. Now we'll have to kill them all."

The cook swooned onto the settee.

The young deputy on the veranda turned at the sound of the door opening behind him. He recognized the Pinkerton. "Leaving so soon?"

"I have to wire the home office for instructions." He adjusted his hat, which he had retrieved from the peg beside the door, and removed a long cigar from inside his coat. "Have you a match?"

The deputy cradled his Winchester in the crook of his left arm and dug one out. Striking it on a porch post, he cupped the flame and held it to the end of the detective's cigar. Suddenly something rigid prodded his stomach. He looked down at the revolver.

"It's much warmer inside," suggested the Pinkerton gently.

CHAPTER 14

Though he tried to look dapper, the witness' blocky five-foot-nine frame lent him the look of a bartender in his black coat and vest and striped trousers. He had a round face and mild eyes inclined to twinkle and a well-kept handlebar, all of which added to the impression, but as he approached the stand and laid an incongruously slender hand atop the Bible proffered by the bailiff, the quickness of his movements gave him away. Ben Thompson—English born, Texas raised, former saloon owner and future Texas Ranger and Austin city marshal—had killed a score of men and would add twelve more to the list before his own death in an ambush by hired assassins in 1884. Asked his occupation, he answered, "Businessman."

General Crandall leaned back against the defense table with his ankles crossed and his hands folded upon his paunch and waited patiently for the excitement triggered by the infamous killer's appearance to die down. He noted that the jurors, who had settled back in their seats after Buffalo Bill's cross-examination, were upright once more, eyes alert and trained on the witness to a man.

At the other table, Julian Scout sat so that he could observe both Crandall and Thompson without turning his head. He looked fresh despite the General's expert negation of his star witness' testimony. He was a better lawyer than he thought himself, Crandall suspected, glad to be facing him before he had a chance to find out how good he was. Bartholomew, the one to watch, looked half asleep, head propped up on his palm and gazing at nothing in particular. None of this damned obsessive taking of notes for either of them, the General thought, eyeing his own partner cramped over a fresh sheet already half filled with shorthand scribble. Since Gannon never bothered to translate the symbols for his benefit, the defender theorized that he was preparing his autobiography.

The room was quiet and all eyes, except for Bartholomew's and

Gannon's, were on him. He let his own gaze drift over to engage Thompson's.

"Mr. Thompson, you were part owner of a saloon in Abilene, Kansas, in 1871, were you not?"

"I was." His speech betrayed nothing of his Yorkshire origins. Contrary to the popular conception of the close-mouthed killer, the reply was anything but sullen; seated with his legs crossed, eyes crinkled to reveal deep laugh lines at the corners, Thompson seemed about to relate an off-color joke. The gallery felt cheated. Crandall sensed this reaction and dismissed it as unimportant.

"That was during James Butler Hickok's term as marshal of that city?"

"It was."

"Was the name of the saloon in which you held part interest the Bull's Head?"

"That's right."

"Was your partner Phil Coe?"

"Yes, sir." His use of the term "sir" was not a sign of subservience, but was merely a gesture of politeness. Calm reserve masked the inner man from the jovial pose like a steel shield.

"The same Phil Coe killed by Hickok on October 5, 1871, as Mr. Scout pointed out to this assembly yesterday?"

"Hickok killed him, right enough."

"Thank you, Mr. Thompson. Now, in your capacity as Coe's partner, did you ever find occasion to enter into dealings with Marshal Hickok?"

"Almost daily."

"Would you describe for this court the nature of said dealings?"

"Each morning Hickok would present himself at the door of the Bull's Head and receive a poke containing a percentage of the house's profits from the previous night's gambling activities."

Scout was up in an instant, but the room was already humming. "Objection! Your Honor, the defense has brought forth not one scrap of evidence to substantiate this calumny."

Crandall presented him with a deadpan. "With my colleague's permission, I will signal when releasing this witness for cross-examination."

Blair said, "He's right, counselor. Objection overruled."

Crandall continued. "To your knowledge, Mr. Thompson, was this common practice among the marshals of Abilene?"

"I can't say from firsthand experience whether it was or wasn't," said the witness. "But that is the way things stood when Phil and me struck a partnership. I am told that Tom Smith, Hickok's predecessor and the town's first law, was not in that habit."

"Objection. Hearsay." This time the prosecutor kept his seat. Blair sustained it.

"Was the Bull's Head the only establishment which subscribed to this . . . arrangement?"

"No. Hickok regularly collected a cut of the winnings from every gambling emporium in Abilene, of which there were considerable, it being a cowtown."

"He received this in addition to his salary as marshal?"

"Yes, as well as fifty percent of all fines collected within the city limits."

Crandall raised his expressive eyebrows. "I never realized enforcing the law could be so profitable." He glimpsed Scout rising and said, "I withdraw that remark, Your Honor. I'm afraid my emotions got the better of me."

"I quite understand your motives, General," the judge responded dryly. "More than you suspect."

The prosecutor sat down, knuckles whitening as he clutched the edge of the table. His opponent had stolen a march on him and left him powerless to combat it.

"At what point, Mr. Thompson," resumed Crandall, "did Coe and Hickok become enemies?"

"I would not say that they were ever friends," Thompson said. "But the final break came when upon my advice Phil refused to pay the marshal one more penny for protection."

"Protection? Protection from what?"

The witness smiled coldly. "Hickok was always vague on that point. When challenged he would sometimes make reference to fires, other times to the possibility of closing down the establishment for ordinance violations. The way he said it, you could take it two ways. But you didn't."

"Assumption and conjecture!" Scout shouted.

"Sustained. Control yourself, Mr. Scout. This is not a public auction." Blair had the response stricken and instructed the jury to disregard it.

Crandall, still leaning against his table, was unperturbed. "What was Marshal Hickok's reaction when told he could expect no more money from the Bull's Head?"

"He turned white. The saloon hadn't opened yet. Hickok and Phil were in front of the bar and I was behind it. I thought he might draw then and there, and laid on top of the bar a sawed-off shotgun I had been holding. He looked from it to me, saw that I was prepared to use it if necessary, and relaxed. Then he said something indelicate and went out. The next day he came in with an order to close down the saloon."

"What reason did he cite for this maneuver?"

"He claimed that our sign violated the ordinance prohibiting public indecency."

"And did it?"

Thompson shrugged. "The bull we had painted on the sign included what might be called a physical exaggeration. We never heard any complaints. But Hickok said if it wasn't changed he'd enforce the order and we'd be out of business."

"Did Hickok hate Phil Coe for refusing to cut him in on the house winnings?"

"Well, that was enough to start something, but the way those two felt about each other had more to do with Phil stealing Hickok's woman."

For the first time since the testimony had begun, Crandall abandoned his relaxed pose and stood upright, as if the answer shocked him. He had an accomplished actor's sense of theater. "Indeed! Tell us about that, Mr. Thompson."

"Hickok had for some time been courting Miss Jessie Hazell when Phil came along and she took up with him. When he found out, the marshal swore he'd kill him."

Crandall gave the murmuring in the gallery time to peak and begin to fade before asking, "Did you hear Hickok deliver this threat?"

"I didn't personally, but it was common knowledge around town."

Controlling himself with an effort, Scout objected on the grounds of hearsay and was sustained. Once again the jurors were asked to put aside something they had heard.

"When this is turned over to them, they're going to spend more time forgetting than remembering," Bartholomew confided to his partner. The prosecutor, pale with suppressed rage, didn't answer.

"What sort of man was Phil Coe?" Crandall inquired.

Thompson answered without pausing. "He was the best and truest friend a man has ever known. A big, strapping fellow, he was as quick with a slap on the back and a joke as Hickok was with a pistol. I consider myself lucky to have been blessed with such a man for my partner."

"When did you first hear that he had been killed?"

"A few days after the event. I had not seen him for three months. My leg was broken and my wife and little boy were badly used when our buggy overturned during a ride across the countryside. We were taken to the Lindell Hotel in Kansas City and there treated for several weeks. I wrote Phil to tell him what had happened, and he wired me three thousand dollars. We were on our way to my mother's home in Austin for a rest when we were overtaken by a party bearing Phil's casket. That was when I learned that Hickok had killed my partner and closed down the Bull's Head."

All trace of good humor had evaporated from Ben Thompson's manner. As he droned on tonelessly, his emotion reflected only in the hard glitter that had replaced the twinkle in his eyes, a chill silence descended like a shroud over the assembly. This was the killer speaking. Crandall sensed this and made use of it.

"What did the members of the funeral procession tell you of the killing?"

"They said that Phil had been celebrating with his friends his intention to leave Abilene with Jessie Hazell when Hickok stepped out of a hotel doorway and shot him in the back at close range with a derringer. When Hickok's own friend, Mike Williams, protested, he shot and killed him too."

"Hearsay!" Scout's chair tipped over as he leaped up, crashing to the floor with an ear-splitting report. "Defense counsel has repeatedly violated the rules of evidence in the interests of forestalling the inevitable. He has attempted time after time to sway the jury through illegal means, and I do not intend to stand for it!" He was leaning so far over the table, supporting himself upon his hands, that he was actually on all fours. His chest was heaving and his face glistened with perspiration.

"Are you finished with your tirade, counselor?" Coming upon the heels of Scout's bellowing, the judge's measured tones fell with greater force than usual.

Scout straightened, suddenly aware of appearing ridiculous. "My apologies to Your Honor and to this court for my unseemly outburst."

Blair was unmoved. Long, bony hands folded beneath his chin, he focused washed-out gray eyes upon each attorney in turn. "The reputations of all counsels involved with this case have inclined me toward leniency. Because of the unorthodox nature of the issues at hand I have overlooked various borderline illegalities which another judge would be swift to staunch. I have issued far more warnings and far fewer punishments than is my usual custom. In return, I have received little but contempt. So hear this: If during the course of this trial either of you should attempt to slip anything past this bench which does not bear directly upon the fate of the accused, I will declare this a mistrial and have that man up on charges before the American Bar Association at the earliest opportunity. If I have not made myself clear please apprise." Neither attorney spoke. He nodded. "Very well. The objection raised by counsel for the prosecution is sustained. All reference to what the witness was told regarding the death of Phil Coe will be stricken from the record. The jury will disregard it. General—"

Permission to proceed was interrupted as a deputy marshal who had been on guard at the door came down the aisle and bent to whisper in Scout's ear. The prosecutor turned his head and whispered back as though asking a question. He nodded and rose.

"My apologies again, Your Honor. Something urgent has come up and I must request a fifteen-minute recess while I attend to it."

"Does it bear upon this case, counselor?"

"I am told it does."

"You have fifteen minutes." The gavel descended.

Accompanied by Bartholomew, Scout followed the deputy into the corridor, where Marshal Burdick greeted him wordlessly with a tissue-wrapped package containing Grace Sargent's yellow bonnet.

CHAPTER 15

A heavy black woman in a brown hooded cloak that covered her from head to foot monk-fashion was standing beside the grim-looking marshal. Before Scout had time to realize the significance of the bundle in Burdick's hands she blurted, "I didn't want to bring him, Mr. Scout, sir. He made me show him what I had. They told me they'd kill Miz Sargent if I was to try and fetch the law." She was shivering violently. It was a moment before the prosecutor recognized the round, creased face in the depths of the hood as that of Grace's cook. Bartholomew, quicker on the uptake, laid a paternal hand on Scout's arm.

"I was on my way to check on the deputies I had guarding Mrs. Sargent's place when I come upon her waddling along with this here clutched in her arms like it was a baby." Burdick raised the package. "When I stepped in front of her she like to of pounded me to a pulp. If I hadn't learned to defend myself in the ring a long time ago she'd of busted my nose. You recollect this here?"

"It's Grace's bonnet." Scout's dead calm seemed to startle the big marshal. He couldn't know of the sick emptiness that had come over the prosecutor upon recognizing the item. "Where is she?"

The cook was crying hysterically. Suddenly the bottom fell out of Scout's reserve and he seized her by the shoulders. *"Where is she?"* The shout rang in the rafters of the corridor. All murmuring inside the courtroom ceased. Automatically the deputy reached in and pulled the door shut.

"Easy, Julian." Bartholomew placed his hands on Scout's own shoulders. His eternal calm seemed to pass into his partner, who relaxed and slackened his grip, finally releasing it altogether. The cook had by this time subsided into a blubbering fit.

"This was inside the bonnet." Burdick handed him a sheet of

light blue notepaper, Grace's stationery. Her handwriting was as clear and firm as if she had been drafting an invitation to tea.

Julian,

Eloise has been chosen to bring you this message because she is the most frightened and the least likely to disobey orders. Although I am inclined to disagree, that is the reasoning of the men who are holding guns on me at this moment. I have been told to write that if you do not dismiss the charges against Jack McCall they will kill me and everyone else in the house. Eloise is to return with your reply by two o'clock.

Love,
Grace

"How many are holding them?" His outward calm had returned, but the paper rattled like a telegraph key in his hands.

"The cook seen two. There might be more, but I doubt it. That don't improve the odds none. I figure they killed my deputies or they wouldn't be in there." Burdick's ham of a face betrayed no emotion.

"Have you any idea who they are?" asked Bartholomew.

"Eloise here gave me a pretty fair description of both of them. The tall Southerner giving the orders sounds like Johnny Varnes from an old wanted dodger I dug up on him. It don't say nothing about a beard, but he could of growed that when things got tight in Deadwood. The other fits the description Mrs. Hope gave us of the one she saw watching the place the other night. I've got a theory about him. Varnes had a partner down in Deadwood name of Tim Brady. I couldn't locate no paper on him, but I'm figuring Varnes is too smart to change horses on the gallop."

Bartholomew said, "But why is he taking this chance? What can he hope to gain?"

"I've got a theory about that too. McCall was going to implicate him in Hickok's killing and backed out. Varnes figures if he's convicted he'll spill everything just to beat the rope. Holding people hostage carries a lesser sentence than murder, and being a fugitive ain't Varnes's style, so maybe my deputies are alive after all. He's boxing the compass." He paused, then, "This might explain that dead Pinkerton one of the city marshal's boys fished out of the river this morning, fellow name of Lucy. He'd been stripped and his face bashed in, but a deputy recognized him anyway. His credentials might have got them inside the house."

"Mother of God!"

The exclamation startled Burdick, who hadn't observed General Crandall opening the courtroom door. All the color had fled the defense attorney's features.

"Who the hell are you?" demanded the marshal, embarrassed by his own jumpiness.

"My esteemed opponent," Scout snarled. But his sarcasm lacked conviction.

"In more ways than one, apparently," agreed Crandall. "I hired the Pinkerton."

The three glared at him. He said, "Don't arrest me yet, Marshal. I instructed my partner to engage a detective for Mrs. Sargent's protection."

"Since when have you been so interested in her welfare?" barked the prosecutor.

"Since it threatened to affect the outcome of this trial. I don't want to win that way. I'll win, but I'll do it on my own, with no outside help."

"Perhaps this is your doing."

Bartholomew said, "Julian, that was uncalled for. Crandall is a reputable—"

The General held up a hand, cutting him off in mid-sentence. He met Scout's gaze. "I fight my battles in the courtroom, counselor. But you've seen how I operate. If I had a hand in this, do you seriously think I'd leave you room to discuss alternatives?"

Scout shook his head, suddenly too tired to think.

"This decision isn't ours alone," suggested his partner. "I vote we take it up with Judge Blair."

Like Scout, the judge was a pipe smoker. Once behind the desk in his book-lined study he seized a charred blob of briar from a stand of more respectable-looking clays and cherrywoods and began stuffing it with black shag from a worn leather pouch. In the bright sunlight streaming through the window he looked even older than he did on the bench, his eyes tired black hollows beneath the shaggy white shelf of his brows. He finished charging the pipe and lit it while Bartholomew briefed him. The attorney might have been quoting an

obscure legal precedent for all the effect his words seemed to have
on Blair.

When Bartholomew was finished, the judge shook out his match
and dropped it into a heavy brass ashtray on the corner of the blot-
ter. He sat back against the high, leather-upholstered back of his
swivel chair, smoking and regarding the faces of Marshal Burdick,
General Crandall, and Orville Gannon, seated, and of Bartholomew
and Scout, the former standing before his desk, his partner a restless
dark profile against the window. Gannon, who had learned of this
latest development along with the judge, reflected neither surprise
nor dismay. Blair wondered how deep his emotionless façade went,
or if it was a façade at all. The black woman's soft sobbing was the
only sound in the room; Burdick, showing more sensitivity than the
judge had believed he possessed, had seated her beside him, where
she could draw upon his stolid presence.

"I would add obstruction of justice to the charge of unlawful incarceration," Blair commented at last. "Mr. Scout, why was I not informed of the threats against you from the beginning?"

Bartholomew answered for him. "Threats are nothing new when
a celebrated case is being tried, Your Honor. We took routine steps
for Mr. Scout's protection and let it go at that. We thought it best
not to bother you with it."

"I like being bothered, Mr. Bartholomew. If I did not I would
never have accepted this assignment. I assume all the necessary pre-
cautions have been taken?" His eyes went to Burdick, who nodded
ponderously.

"I've got all the deputies I can spare watching the house from
cover. They're instructed to keep cover and do nothing unless they
try to leave the house."

"And if they do?"

"One of them is to follow along while the others get word back to
me. I don't want any hostages caught in crossfire if I can help it."

"May I see the message?"

Burdick drew the blue slip of paper from the package on his lap
and leaned forward to place it in the judge's outstretched hand. Blair
read it, holding it at arm's length. He had left his spectacles in the
courtroom.

"You're certain this is Mrs. Sargent's hand, Mr. Scout?"

"Yes, yes." The strain was beginning to show. Ignoring his curtness, the judge turned to Crandall.

"How did these people find out you were hiring a Pinkerton?"

"Not from me," put in Gannon. "I mentioned it to no one but agent Lucy."

Crandall said, "I instructed Mr. Gannon to engage a detective during his visit to my cell. There were other prisoners in the block. It's possible we were overheard."

"That could be," agreed Burdick. "We gave up trying to stamp out the grapevine a long time ago. My figuring is that Varnes or someone representing him came in and spread some money around, looking for information. Among the prisoners, of course."

"Of course." Blair spoke archly. "How would the defense answer this threat?"

The General sat with his chin on his chest and fingers laced across his swollen middle. "As I told the others earlier, I'd rather not win on the merits of someone else's efforts. But the decision is not mine to make."

Orville Gannon said nothing. His eyes were flat discs behind the lenses of his spectacles. Blair gave up trying to read what was behind them.

"Does Your Honor have any suggestions?" Bartholomew asked.

"This is Marshal Burdick's investigation. Marshal?"

The big man shrugged a massive shoulder. "That's Scout's lady friend in there."

Blair shook his head. "Dropping the case against the defendant under these circumstances would lay us all open to charges of influence. He can, however, ask to be replaced, in which event I will be obliged to declare a mistrial and start all over again with a fresh deck." He frowned at his own choice of images. Only a handful of his card-playing friends knew of the judge's affinity for poker.

"Well," said Crandall, consulting his watch, "someone had better decide soon. It's quarter past one."

All eyes swung to Scout. He fidgeted, finally meeting the marshal's gaze. "You're the expert. What would you do?"

"That's easy," said Burdick. "Lie."

"Lie?" The prosecutor echoed him as if the word had no meaning for him.

"Tell him you'll drop the charges. Buy time. When you come down to it, time's the only weapon we have."

"What makes you think I'd be lying?"

"Perhaps I haven't made myself clear." Blair's voice was cold. "Should you decide to dismiss the charges under duress, I shall take steps to see that you never plead another case in any court."

Burdick watched Scout quietly. "I been standing on this side of a badge long enough to know a sticker from a quitter. You wouldn't knuckle under any quicker than I would."

After a moment the prosecutor said, "Suppose I buy you the time you need. What will you do with it?"

"I'll have to ask you to trust me there."

"Marshal." Scout turned his back to the window, a tall man whose sagging shoulders took the place of features blacked out against the glare and made up for the misleading blandness of his tone. "The woman I hope to marry is locked up in that house with at least two killers. Give me one good reason why I shouldn't know what you're going to do about it."

The lawman answered without hesitation. "Because I don't know myself."

Silence lay heavy in the room. Even the cook had stopped crying, her tears glistening on her puffy cheeks as she watched Scout. At length he nodded.

"Do what you have to, Marshal." He pushed away from the window.

"What about you?" Burdick rose.

"I'm going to do what the taxpayers pay me for: Pull every legal string I know to see that a murderer like McCall hangs."

"That's off the record, of course," put in Crandall.

In spite of himself Scout smiled. "Of course."

"What time is it?" Tim Brady asked, coming into the entrance hall, where Varnes had moved the hostages because of the big windows that looked out upon the street.

Varnes, occupying a satin-upholstered sofa opposite the one in which sat Grace Sargent, Dora Hope and the four remaining servants, inspected his pocket watch. The captured deputy was seated on the floor near the others, gagged with a handkerchief and bound with the cord from a sash weight. "One-twenty," said the Southerner. "There's plenty of time yet."

"You don't reckon she went for the law, do you?"

"I don't reckon she didn't." He met Brady's stare. "I told you at the start there was no hope of us walking away from this free men. I gave you the choice of spending a year or two behind bars or dodging the hangman for the rest of your life. You made it."

"Yeah, but things are different now."

"You made them different when you killed that deputy. If you'd taken him hostage like I told you, we'd have reason to bargain. Now we're facing a murder charge no matter which way we turn."

"You didn't feel that way when you told me to kill the Pinkerton."

"I also told you to fix it so the body couldn't be identified and linked to us. You did do that?" He looked at him questioningly.

"I ditched his clothes and messed his face up good. His own mother wouldn't know him."

"I'm not so sure. In any case it no longer matters."

"So why go through with it? Why didn't we just light a shuck instead of sending the nigger woman out with that note?"

"We wouldn't have made a mile. With hostages we may be able to bargain our way onto a ferry and head for Canada. The note may make them think we haven't killed anyone. The cook can't tell them about the dead deputy because she doesn't know about him. If they found out we'd killed a fellow lawman, they'd burn us out and shoot down everyone who steps out the door, hostages or no hostages."

"In other words, we're bluffing."

"In other words, yes." Varnes smiled bitterly. "Hickok would love it, the poker-playing son of a bitch."

Brady was studying Grace Sargent's ankle where a crumpled fold in the hem of her skirt exposed two inches of stocking above her shoe top. Noticing the angle of his gaze, she rearranged the material to cover it. Varnes noticed too.

"There'll be time enough for that on board the ferry," he told his partner. "Get back in the kitchen and keep an eye on the rear of the house. Or maybe you'd rather be up to your ears in her petticoats when the law gets here."

"It'd almost be worth it," leered Brady.

CHAPTER 16

Two unexplained recesses had raised the atmosphere in the court-room to a fever pitch of anticipation, which was quickly extinguished as Crandall resumed his interrogation of Ben Thompson by going back over ground already covered to refresh the jury's memory.

"One more question, Mr. Thompson," he said, once the details of the deceased's relationship with Phil Coe were fixed. "As you know, my client is on trial for the slaying of James Butler Hickok. Based upon your dealings with the man you knew as Wild Bill, how do you feel about that?"

Thompson stared at McCall, who jerked his head up to return his gaze. There was nothing mild about the witness' eyes now.

"If my leg weren't broken when Phil was killed," he said, bringing his attention back to the attorney, "that'd be me sitting there in irons."

Scout took advantage of the excited murmuring prompted by Thompson's comment to confer with Bartholomew. "There's a mine of material to choose from," he said, arranging the clippings he needed from the dusty pile on the table. "Where shall I start?"

"Jessie Hazell was nothing more than a prostitute. You can chip away at that statue Thompson's erected to Coe by asking him if he knew she moved in with his partner after dumping Hickok."

"No good. That reduces their shoot-out to an argument over the affections of a whore, and where does that leave our heroic lawman? I think I'll go directly to the source."

He rose. "Your final comment interested me very much, Mr. Thompson," he began, striking a casual pose with hands in pockets. "You weren't indulging in idle bombast, were you?"

"I never have." The witness appeared wary.

"Just how many men have you killed, Mr. Thompson?"

"Objection." Crandall kept his seat. "The witness is not on trial."

"Your Honor, I am merely exploring Mr. Thompson's answer to defense counsel's last question," said Scout.

"Objection overruled. The witness is instructed to answer."

"I never killed anyone who didn't deserve it."

"Ah, yes, the killer's credo." The prosecutor strolled around in front of the table. "However, that is not the issue."

"In the war—"

"Let's not count the war. How many men have you killed in civilian life, Mr. Thompson? That should help keep the number within the bounds of credibility." When the witness hesitated, "Would you say five, for example?"

"I would say I've killed five, yes."

"Would you say six? Eight? How about ten? Or would twenty be closer to the truth? Answer me, Mr. Thompson. Have you killed twenty men?" His voice had risen steadily until he was shouting.

"Yes!" bellowed the man in the box, and when he realized that the other had stopped shouting he sank in upon himself, embarrassed for having lost control.

"You seem proud of it, Mr. Thompson." Scout's tone was oily.

"Objection!" barked Crandall.

"Sustained. My warning stands, counselor."

The prosecutor inclined his head in an apologetic bow. But his eyes remained on Thompson. "In 1856, when you were thirteen years old, did you stand trial in Austin, Texas, for shooting another boy in the backside with a shotgun?"

The question caught Thompson offguard. "Loaded with mustard seed!" he retorted, after an instant.

"Was a conviction obtained?"

"Yes, but the jury recommended clemency and the governor issued a pardon. It was a schoolboy prank."

"A painful one, I would imagine." Scout went on. "Years later, were you the subject of a manhunt in New Orleans for having killed a Frenchman in a duel?"

"You can't prove that." The witness' eyes were dangerous.

"Do you deny that you were sought for the slaying?"

"It was said that I had killed the man in a fair fight after I had observed him forcing unwelcome attentions upon a young lady aboard a coach. I was forced to hide out in the Sicilian quarter until friends helped me out of town."

"Do you deny that you killed the Frenchman?"

Crandall popped up. "He doesn't have to answer that."

The judge leaned down toward Thompson. "Do you plead the Fifth Amendment?"

Thompson glanced toward Crandall, who nodded almost imperceptibly. Scout regretted not having placed himself between them. The witness nodded.

"Answer yes or no, Mr. Thompson," Blair directed. "The recorder takes no note of gestures."

"Yes."

"Let the record show that the witness declines to answer on the grounds of self-incrimination."

"I have no objections," said Scout blandly. "There is much more here, as Mr. Thompson well knows." He glanced at his notes. "Shortly after the outbreak of hostilities between North and South, while serving the Confederacy under Colonel John R. Taylor at Fort Clark, New Mexico Territory, were you arrested for shooting and killing a mess sergeant during a quarrel and attacking a lieutenant who tried to stop you?"

"Your Honor, the witness has admitted to having slain a certain number of men." Crandall's tone belonged to a disappointed headmaster. "I see no reason for his having to do so again in this tedious fashion. For that matter, I see no reason for this entire line of questioning. What bearing does it have upon his testimony?"

Countered Scout, "Your Honor, defense counsel has asked Thompson to render a sullied picture of the deceased's character. I question the witness' ability to make such a moral judgment based upon his own dubious past."

Blair considered for a moment before responding. "I cannot in good conscience allow you to continue this line, counselor. A man who has killed is not necessarily a perjurer. Besides, we seem to be straying rather far from the issue at hand, which is the guilt or innocence of the accused. Recorder, strike everything after the witness' response to the question, 'Have you killed twenty men?'"

The paper in the prosecutor's hands tore loudly. Enraged by the impertinence, Blair snatched up his gavel. Before he could strike it:

"I'm sorry, Your Honor," Scout said hastily. "It was a nervous reaction." The judge nodded abruptly and sat back.

As Scout turned from the bench to deposit his notes atop the prosecution table, Bartholomew was alarmed at his partner's expression.

Tension had drawn his features into a caricature. His hands shook as he absentmindedly straightened up the rent pages. But the face he presented the court a moment later was serenely confident.

"Phil Coe was the greatest man who ever lived, is that right, Mr. Thompson?"

"Well, I wouldn't go so far as to say that." The witness was condescending. His contentment had returned with the locking away of his past.

"Oh, but you did," chided the prosecutor. "Asked by General Crandall your opinion of Coe's character, you called him 'the best and truest friend a man has ever known.' It's in the record if you don't remember."

"Perhaps I said something of the sort." Thompson shifted in his seat. "I would amend it to say that he was the best friend I ever had. Anything more would be an exaggeration."

"Are you given to exaggerate?"

"Objection!"

"I withdraw the question," Scout said, before the judge could sustain. "What would you say if I told you that Phil Coe was incarcerated at Galveston, Texas, during the late war for impersonating an officer?"

"I would say that you are a damned liar!" thundered the witness.

"You would then be guilty of perjury, Mr. Thompson, for records show that you shared Coe's cell after you were arrested for desertion." The prosecutor was moving forward, boxing him in.

"I'd forgotten. It's been twelve years."

"You seem to have no trouble remembering how long it's been. Unlike you, Coe was a civilian. Did he flee to Mexico until the end of the war to avoid conscription?"

"You tell me."

"No, Mr. Thompson, you tell me. That is what you are here to do."

"I don't know where Phil was. Right after I was released I helped capture the *Harriet Lane* at Galveston and assisted in the destruction of other Union vessels in the harbor. Then my regiment was ordered to Louisiana, where we routed Pyron at La Fourche and my brother Billy and I became separated from the company. We kept stumbling over dead men and horses. My leg had been injured when my horse fell on it and after we located the rest of the command I was laid up for weeks while it healed. After that we transferred to Colonel Ford's outfit and were assigned patrol duty east of the Rio Grande. I didn't hear from Phil all that time and had no idea if he was even alive."

"I agree that it was a hectic period for you. The record shows that you were placed in the guardhouse for attacking yet another sergeant, this time with your crutch. Had it not broken, your toll thus far would be twenty-one."

"Objection!" Crandall spoke up harshly. Actually, he wasn't as angry with the prosecutor for the derogatory comment as he was with his witness for parading his record as a Confederate soldier before a northern court.

"Sustained. I've ruled against this line, counselor."

Scout adjusted his tack. "In Abilene, did Marshal Hickok ever threaten you or Coe in so many words that failure to turn over a portion of the Bull's Head's winnings would result in its being burned or closed down?"

"He was clear enough about it," was the sullen reply.

"That isn't what I asked."

"He didn't say so in those words. Hickok was too cagey for that."

"As the reigning lawman in Abilene, wasn't it Hickok's duty to protect the businesses as well as the citizens within his jurisdiction from harm?"

"Yes, but he was paid to do that from the taxes."

"Did you and Coe pay taxes?"

"We bought a license to operate, which amounts to the same thing."

"Not precisely, Mr. Thompson. Licensing requires a set fee to be paid on a regular basis. The amount doesn't vary unless the city charter is amended to allow for the increased or decreased cost of living. Taxes, which in most parts of the world are levied against income, are based on percentages and rise or fall with the principal. Couldn't it be said that the percentage of winnings that yours and the other gambling establishments in Abilene were required to surrender to the marshal constituted an income tax, in return for which you received the protection to which you were entitled?"

"It could not! It was extortion, pure and simple!"

"So *you* say. But then your opinion could hardly be termed impartial, could it, Mr. Thompson?" The prosecutor had his hands on the railing and was leaning over the witness, his face closer to Thompson's than that of any other the killer had allowed to live.

"Your Honor, the prosecutor is being argumentative. This is not a Harvard debate."

"Sustained. But leave my alma mater out of this, General." The judge smiled thinly.

"You intimated earlier that your refusal to share your profits with the marshal's office resulted in a threat to close the Bull's Head," resumed Scout, uncowed by Blair's ruling. "What evidence do you have to substantiate this claim?"

"Ask anyone who was there. They'll tell you." Thompson's serenity was once again a thing of the past. His forehead was dark.

"No one else was there, Mr. Thompson."

"Are you calling me a liar?" Cold death lurked behind the gunman's retort.

"Yes, Mr. Thompson," said Scout. "A liar is exactly what I'm calling you." His voice rose. "An hour ago, in that very chair, you told General Crandall and this court that the Bull's Head was closed when Phil Coe refused Hickok his daily stipend. You said that you and Coe and the marshal were alone in the room. Now you claim that others were present. Somewhere you are lying, Mr. Thompson. I have a roomful of people and the court record to bear witness to that. What proof have you?"

"I meant afterward, when Hickok came around with the order to close. There were a dozen witnesses at least."

"Was anything said at that time about funds refused Hickok?"

"Well, no, but everyone knew—"

"Do you deny that the sign before your establishment violated the ordinance against public indecency?"

"Technically—"

"Technicalities are all that concerns this court. Would you agree that as city marshal, empowered to uphold the laws of Abilene and the State of Kansas, James Butler Hickok was acting within his rights when he ordered you and Phil Coe to change your sign or be closed?"

Thompson was trapped. He kept silent as long as possible, obviously hoping that Crandall would object. When it was evident that no such reprieve was forthcoming, he fixed the prosecutor with a look of raw hatred.

"Yes," he snarled. "I suppose I'd have to."

Scout thanked him abruptly and said that there were no more questions. When the prosecutor was back in his seat, Bartholomew leaned close to his ear and whispered, "I don't remember him saying anything about he and Coe being alone with Hickok when they refused to pay."

"Fortunately, neither did he."

Crandall waived redirect, upon which Thompson, excused, tramped briskly toward the gate separating the principals from the spectators. On his way through it he paused.

"Do yourself a favor and stay away from Texas." The whisper was so low that only the prosecutor heard it. Then he was gone.

"Call your next witness, counselor," Blair told the General.

"Your Honor, we call the defendant, Jack McCall."

CHAPTER 17

The rifle was a full Sharps Big Fifty, equipped with a descending breechblock and set trigger and a range, if the tales of some buffalo hunters were to be credited, of a thousand yards. Certainly it was good for six hundred. Anyone who hankered to shoot farther than that was dreaming anyway. Pound for pound it was the best long-range target gun ever invented, which suited Deputy U. S. Marshal Walter Donaldson down to the ground, because he was the best long-range target shooter ever born. So he styled himself, and the sharpshooting medals in his war chest and dozens of blue ribbons garnered from every turkey shoot between Bismarck and Wichita bore him out.

He didn't look the part. Small-boned, with a narrow, stubble-bearded face and watery eyes behind thick spectacles, he might have been a clerk fallen on hard times but for his expensive fur hat and shaggy, ankle-length coat, bulky attire designed for sitting or standing for hours in the freezing cold. He was putting them to maximum use now, lying full-length on his stomach upon a rooftop in the blowing snow half a block to the rear of the Sargent mansion. His cheek rested on the smooth wooden stock of the Sharps while he kept his bare trigger hand warm beneath his left armpit.

He had let pass a hundred chances at his target, a pistol-toter in shabby clothes and a derby who kept coming to the kitchen window to peer out. Burdick had ordered Donaldson to hold his fire until signaled. Presumably, this would be the task of the laborer whom the deputy had spotted tarring a roof across the street from the house with the aid of a smoking smudge pot. Though he was too far away for positive identification, the man's ponderous build and the way he moved told Donaldson that this was Harry Wildfire, a full-blooded Shoshone the marshal sometimes hired for jobs his deputies refused.

Outlined clearly against the gray sky, he offered a tempting target if anyone in the house became suspicious.

Donaldson had no idea who was in the house or what they were doing, nor did he care. The army had taught him not to ask questions of his superiors, and the lesson had stuck. He only knew that he was there to kill the first male that showed himself at a window once the signal was given.

He had no qualms about this. Burdick had called upon him to do much the same thing more times than he could remember, and he had yet to fail the marshal, despite the fact that there was no love lost between the two. He had nothing but contempt for the head lawman, who detested Donaldson for his record of kills, but who never hesitated to make use of his talents whenever they were needed. Yet the deputy had never considered resigning, for he knew of no other honest work that would let him do what he did best, and the risks involved in most illegal enterprises with which he was familiar were prohibitive. He possessed no conscience, and suspected that this much-touted emotion was the invention of politicians and lawmen like Burdick designed to prevent crime and save them the trouble of apprehending criminals. The taking of life meant no more to him than the opening of a can of sardines.

In short, Walter Donaldson was an assassin, perhaps the best of his kind.

"It's five of two. Where is your cook, Mrs. Sargent?"

There was no tension in John Varnes's voice, but Grace could feel it nonetheless, thick as must in the air between them. She fought to keep it out of her own manner.

"Eloise has never been on time for anything in her life."

"That's unfortunate. She won't want to miss her mistress' funeral."

They were seated across from each other in the entrance hall as before. Varnes had returned his partner's Smith & Wesson in favor of his own Remington, recaptured from the trussed deputy. As the minutes had crawled past, the nearly tangible odor of fear in the room had retreated before boredom, but with two o'clock approaching rapidly they had traded places again. The hostages' eyes were restless. All but those of Dora Hope.

For nearly an hour, Grace's mother had sat motionless on the sofa, eyes focused straight ahead, her face a blank slab. She bothered Varnes. Fear in all its normal manifestations he could handle, but there was no predicting what a person suffering from deep shock would do next. He had decided that she would be the first one he'd shoot the moment something went wrong. He looked from her to the daughter, who was watching him, and he knew that she had been reading his thoughts.

"My neck is already in the noose, Mrs. Sargent," he explained. "My partner has seen to that. One murder or eight, they can only drop me through the trap once."

"Why don't you stop playing games?" She spoke bitterly, her words tumbling out in a rush. "You're going to kill us all anyway. You said so."

Her mother's hand squeezed hers. Alarmed for her mental state, Grace shot her a quick glance and was surprised when the older woman's eyes responded. She was cautioning her daughter—not at all the reaction of a person paralyzed with fright.

Varnes hadn't noticed the exchange. "I said what I said to frighten you. I didn't want anyone thinking we didn't mean business. You will live if you cooperate."

"There are degrees of life, Mr. Varnes." Encouraged by her mother's strength, she smiled wickedly at the ripple of surprise that passed across his aristocratic features. "Yes, I know who you are. My mother's interest in crimes of violence hasn't been lost upon me. I put it together when your partner said something about your hiring people to do your killing for you."

"You were talking about degrees of life." He had regained his composure in an instant.

"There is a degree beyond which one's own life is worth nothing. Will I care about living after you've turned me over to your partner aboard the boat, as you said you would?"

He lowered his voice. "As I've already explained, what I say and what I do are often very different from each other. As you may have noticed, my partner has a short attention span. In order to keep his mind upon what is important it is necessary from time to time to dangle a bright bauble before his eyes. To his thinking at least, you sparkle sufficiently to get him down to the river."

"Then what? He'll kill you if you break your promise."

"He won't kill me."

"How can you be so sure? He didn't waste any time on that poor man out back."

"He won't be able to kill me."

She stared at him while his meaning sank in. Then, "Why should you bother? You could be just saying that to get me to cooperate."

"I could," he said. "But then you'll never know unless you cooperate."

After a moment his eyes returned to the front window, beyond which a heavy figure enveloped in a voluminous hooded cloak was hobbling up the walk. The clock in the parlor struck two.

"History is made, Mrs. Sargent," said Varnes, rising. "Your cook is punctual."

Walter Donaldson was blowing on the fingers of his ungloved right hand when the roofer working opposite the mansion stood up and swung his smudge pot in a wide circle around his head, describing a smoky halo that hung there for an instant before the wind tore it to shreds. If that wasn't the signal, Harry Wildfire had discovered a new way of spreading tar. The deputy used his thumb to smear the glare off the Sharps's front sight and drew an unhurried bead on the house.

At that moment, the heel of a pudgy hand rubbed frost off the kitchen window and a moustachioed face beneath a derby was pressed against the glass.

Tim Brady frowned at the bleak scenery out back and wished he were somewhere else. He knew where that somewhere else was, and who should be sharing it with him. Every time he thought about her he was transported to that doorway across the street, watching her peeling shadow. He had never been with a woman like that, and the thought of it made his neck burn and his hands grow slimy.

He was thinking about how it would be on the boat when the window exploded.

"Stay where you are!" Varnes barked, from his position against the wall on the other side of the door. The warning was unnecessary, for none of the hostages had moved. He waited until the brass door knocker sounded tentatively, and then, gripping his revolver in one hand, he pulled the door open with the other.

He was preparing to yank the cook inside when glass tinkled in the distance, followed instantly by a thunderous report.

In spite of his bulky coat, the recoil of Donaldson's Sharps was like a roundhouse to his shoulder. He accounted for it instinctively and didn't miss.

The bullet struck Tim Brady at a sixty-degree angle downward, caving in his face, blazing through the cerebrum (at which point he ceased to know or care what was happening to him), severing the pons Varolii and the centers of sensation, destroying the cerebellum and the victim's balance, and taking out the entire back of his skull upon exit. Its speed undiminished, the slug smashed through the heavy oaken floor near the base of the opposite wall, whistled through the dank air of the basement, splintered a wooden crate, pierced the mortar separating two stones in the foundation, and plowed through twelve feet of earth before stopping. So swiftly had it traveled that Brady, lifted off his feet by the impact, was still in the air when it ground to a halt. He came down dead.

Disregarding the ladies present, John Varnes cursed, for he knew immediately what the noises meant. But his reactions were faster than his judgment and he swung in the direction of the kitchen, taking his revolver from the hostages and the newcomer. Even as he did it he realized his mistake and began to turn back when the cook's cloak flew open and the muzzle of a sawed-off shotgun tickled the back of his neck.

"Your brains would just about reach the wall from here," said Marshal Burdick.

Silence roared as the marshal, looking like an armed monk in the cowled garment, removed the Remington from Varnes's raised left hand. Then something broke inside Dora Hope and out poured a flood of bitter tears.

CHAPTER 18

"No news yet. I'm sorry, Julian."

Scout nodded jerkily as Bartholomew, returning from a brief conference with the deputy marshal at the rear of the room, slid into his seat beside the prosecutor.

"She's all right," said Scout, without conviction.

"Nothing can happen to her while her mother's around. She won't even tolerate snuff in her house." The forced witticism fell on deaf ears and Bartholomew turned his attention to the witness box, where Jack McCall had just been sworn in. Watching his partner in his present state was too painful.

"Your Honor," said Crandall, his voice stiff with indignation, "if a man is innocent until proven guilty, why is my client chained like an animal? How can the jury be expected to render a fair verdict in the presence of what must appear tangible evidence of guilt?"

Blair was terse. "It is understood that the defendant's shackles have no bearing upon his guilt or innocence. The fact that he has once attempted escape makes them necessary."

"Your Honor, I object to the bench's reference to an incident not at issue in this court."

"Overruled. Do not attempt to delay these proceedings any further, counselor."

"Why is he testifying?" Scout asked his partner. "I shouldn't even have to cross-examine. One look at him is worth a guilty verdict."

Bartholomew said, "McCall must have insisted."

"They should build a statue to his arrogance. It'd be sixty feet high and made of brass."

The defendant sat with his manacled hands gripping his knees and the same sullen look on his face he had worn throughout the trial. His sandy hair, freshly pomaded that morning, had come loose and tumbled over his neanderthal forehead. The crossed eye was prominent and red from rubbing. He had a cold.

Crandall wasted no time asking his first question. He wanted to get it over with. "Mr. McCall, you've sat through these proceedings and have heard the evidence presented by both sides. Have you anything to say about what's come to light?"

The defendant responded in a harsh voice accustomed to bellowing, his misaligned eyes roving the courtroom. "Yes, you're damned right, I got plenty to say. Years ago at Rock Creek that killer Hickok murdered my younger brother Andy with a hoe. I swore then and there I'd kill Wild Bill for it, and I have. I been following him around for years just waiting for the right chance."

In the moment following McCall's opening statement, the decorum Judge Blair had struggled so hard to maintain throughout three days of testimony fell apart. The judge's busy gavel was drowned beneath scores of excited conversations, shouts, and bounding feet as journalists sitting on deadline hastened down the aisle toward the nearest telegraph office. "You tell the bastards, Buffalo Curly!" bawled a masculine voice from the back of the room. Rows away, Lorenzo Hickok boiled to his feet with fists clenched. Coloring, Blair pointed with his gavel and the voice's owner was hustled out by the capable bailiff. Hickok sat back down. The judge spent five more minutes restoring order.

"I have no doubt that had the framers of the Constitution been present in this courtroom during that display, the words 'speedy and public trial' would never have appeared in that document," he informed the gallery huffily. "I will not require more than another to clear the premises."

"Would you care to elaborate on the circumstances of your brother's death, Mr. McCall?" asked Crandall, in the subdued atmosphere which followed Blair's admonition.

"I heard it said here that Wild Bill had it out with the McCanles gang at Rock Creek when they raided the stagecoach stop," McCall began. "Well, the truth is that there never was no McCanles gang and no raid. Dave McCanles, who run the station, was bushwhacked by Wild Bill along with his cousin and young son and a hired hand named Jim Gordon. They was unarmed."

"Objection!" said Scout. "Aside from being irrelevant, this reeks of hearsay."

"The accused is offering testimony in his own defense, counselor." Blair was still somewhat agitated. "You will have the opportunity to challenge his statements in cross-examination. Objection overruled."

The prosecution sat down, his face twitching.

"Please continue," Crandall urged his client.

"The main reason Wild Bill hated McCanles was McCanles, who was his boss, was always calling him Duck Bill on account of his upper lip that stuck out. My brother Andy and me—we was just kids —we lived near the station and we thought it was pretty funny, him being called Duck Bill. One day we was passing the station on our way to the fishing hole when we seen Hickok, and Andy said, 'Howdy, Mr. Duck Bill.' Joking like, you know kids.

"I never seen anyone get so mad as Hickok done when Andy called him that. He grabbed a hoe from in front of the building and took out after him. His legs was twice as long as Andy's—it didn't take him no time at all to run him to ground and hit him over the head with that hoe. Andy never come to."

Anticipating the spectators' reaction, Blair banged his gavel before it could get started. A wave of barely suppressed excitement swept through the gallery.

Scout rose, recognizing the uselessness of his motion even as he made it. "Your Honor, if this story is true, why has the defense brought forth no witnesses to substantiate it?"

Crandall raised his animated eyebrows. "I would remind counsel for the prosecution that the burden of proof in a criminal case is on the accuser, not the accused."

"I suppose counsel for the defense has suggestions on how to go about proving a negative?"

"Any assistance I could offer would be construed as collusion." The General spoke silkily.

"Enough!" The judge's gavel punctuated the exclamation. "You're overruled, counselor. Please sit down."

"Why didn't you go to the authorities after your brother was killed?" Crandall asked McCall.

"What authorities? I told you, Rock Creek was a stagecoach stop. There was nary a sheriff or a justice of the peace within a hundred miles."

"And shortly thereafter Hickok became involved in his so-called showdown with McCanles and left Nebraska. You grew up and drifted into Deadwood, where you ran into Hickok once again. What happened then?"

The big man in shackles shrugged. On him the gesture looked sinister. "Nothing much. I seen him once or twice around town and in No. 10, and played poker with him once. He didn't recognize me. He cleaned me out and had the gall to offer me six bits. I told him what he could do with it and left."

"Did you at any time prior to the afternoon of August second draw a firearm to kill Hickok?"

"No, I did not."

"What happened on the afternoon of August second?"

Benches creaked. Every person in the room was leaning forward to hear what Jack McCall had to say. The defendant was hunched over with his elbows resting on his knees, dry-washing his big scarred hands in the gulf between. The rasping sound his calluses made reached into every corner. His close-cropped head was cocked to one side as if he were listening to an inner voice.

"I knowed Hickok would be in No. 10 because he always was at that time, playing poker at the center table. But I didn't have no idea of killing him, on account of he always sat facing the door and if he seen me come in after I got so mad at him the night before, he'd be ready for me. I didn't have no money, he'd cleaned me out like I said. I figured I'd watch the game for a while and see if I could get a drink or two by promising to swamp out after the place closed.

"Even when I seen that Hickok wasn't facing the door, I didn't plan to kill him. He was just too damned fast to fool with. He didn't notice me when I come in, on account of he was losing and in a bad mood about it. He started an argument with Cap'n Massey, who was sitting across from him. Something about the deadwood—I wasn't paying too much attention. Anyway, I got nervous on account of how mad he was and he might see me and figure I was there to beef with him over our card game. I started out the back door. Then something come over me."

He swept a nervous hand across his mouth, callus scraping against the beginnings of coarse stubble. His gaze was directed at the same section of floor he had been watching for days.

"I can't explain it," he continued. "Maybe it was because the argument was still going and no one seemed to have noticed me.

Whatever. I turned around and come back to stand behind Wild Bill.

"I think he must of seen my reflection in his whiskey glass and got suspicious. He went for one of his pistols, but he was sitting down and I had the advantage on him. I pulled my pistol out of my pocket and let him have it in the head before he could kill me. Then I got out in a hurry, because the place was starting to fill up with his friends."

"Once again, Mr. McCall," said the General, amid the hubbub erupting in the courtroom. "James Butler Hickok realized you were behind him and attempted to produce his weapon first."

"That's right."

"Then it was self-defense."

"Yes."

"The penalties for perjury must look pretty soft when you're sitting on a charge of first-degree murder," Scout remarked to Bartholomew, leaning close and raising his voice to be heard over the pandemonium. Blair's gavel was working like a Gatling gun.

"What's your attack?" shouted his partner.

"This." Scout pulled a manila folder from the stack of documents and opened it in front of Bartholomew. The older attorney studied it for a moment, then turned to regard his partner with something approaching awe.

"I received the letter from Cheyenne a week ago," said Scout. "A lot of crank material came in that day, so I didn't bother saying anything about it. I checked it out anyway. The affidavits arrived in this morning's packet. Surprise." He smiled faintly. His mind was elsewhere.

Batholomew said nothing. The prosecutor glanced at him curiously. His partner's eyes were directed beyond his shoulder. He turned to see the court-assigned deputy marshal approaching with a broad grin on his youthful face.

CHAPTER 19

"Where is Eloise?"

Grace was standing in the entrance hall trying to do up the cord of her maroon wrap and getting it hopelessly tangled. Marshal Burdick, having helped load a wagon with a handcuffed and sullen John Varnes and what was left of Tim Brady, was just re-entering the mansion with his shotgun dangling at his side. He realized suddenly that he was still wearing the cook's cloak, took it off hurriedly and draped it over the arm of the settee.

"I stashed her with a matron at the jail. Where are you going?" He stepped forward to help her with the cord. His thick fingers were no better suited to the task.

"I have to get to court and tell Julian I'm all right. Damn the thing! Oh, I'm sorry, Marshal." Her hand flew to her mouth.

His astonished grin cracked the flesh at the corners of his eyes. "No need," he said. "Damn, but I admire a woman who knows how to cuss. Scout's lucky he saw you first. Don't worry about him. I sent someone to give him the word." He became solemn. "You want me to fetch a nurse for your mother?"

She shook her head. "She's upstairs, resting. One of the maids is with her if she needs anything. The other one quit just now. I can't say I blame her." She got the cord undone and began to tie it correctly. "You wouldn't understand, Marshal, but what happened here today may have been the best thing for Mother, Lord knows why. I haven't seen her let go like that in two years. It's a healthy sign."

"You're right, I don't understand." Then he grinned again. "But with your permission, I'll come by someday soon and ask her."

Grace smiled at him, surprised. "Marshal, are you planning to court my mother?"

"With your permission, ma'am," he said. "She reminds me of my late wife. Not that she looks anything like her, but one time when I got back from town I saw the old lady shooing a six-hundred-pound black bear out of the kitchen with a broom. I can picture Mrs. Hope doing that. Damned if I can't."

"I warn you, she doesn't hold with tobacco in any form."

He was silent for a moment, thinking about it. Then, "How does she feel about hard liquor?"

"She's been known to sip brandy on occasion. For medicinal purposes only."

"Well," he said, "it's a start."

A shrill scream brought their heads swinging in the direction of the kitchen. "That's the housekeeper," Grace whispered. Burdick was already moving toward the sound, shotgun leveled. At the door he paused and backed away.

Walter Donaldson and the deputy Burdick had untied after subduing Varnes came in carrying a corpse in a heavy canvas coat. A star glittered on its breast. There was something else on the breast that no longer glittered. Grace turned her head away quickly.

"You dumb bastards!" rasped the marshal. "Don't you know better than to carry a thing like that through the house? Why didn't you take it around outside like the other one?"

The young deputy with the beard was pale and grave. "Beg pardon, Marshal, but the hell with you. He was my pal and he was welcome enough anywhere when he was alive. Being dead don't change nothing."

"Where'd you find him?"

"In a pile of snow out back. Son of a bitch didn't even have the decency to bury him proper."

"What'd you expect, flowers? Get him the hell out of here." He watched grimly as they bore their stiffening burden out the door. "I had myself buffaloed into thinking they'd leave my boys alone." His voice was scarcely audible. "Funny, dead like that he don't look much more than twenty. Maybe he wasn't. Maybe none of them are. Maybe I ought to retire sooner than I figured."

The Greek handyman came in from the veranda. "They said to tell you they're ready, Marshal."

Burdick nodded. "Can I get you a cab, Mrs. Sargent? I'm sorry I can't offer you a ride."

"No, thank you." She tugged loose the cord securing her wrap.

"As long as someone's going to tell Julian, I think I'll stay home with Mother. I don't want to distract him."

He looked at her. "That ain't as easy as it sounds."

"I know," she said. The garment slid slowly from her shoulders.

"He's a good man. You're lucky, too. You're both lucky." He paused. "I hate to leave you with that mess in the kitchen. I can send someone back to take care of it."

"I'm afraid one more strange face would send the rest of the staff packing. We can manage, Marshal. This isn't the first violent death we've had in this house."

"You ought to sell it. Well, good-bye." He went out years older than he had been coming in. Grace stood listening as the horses leaned into the traces and bore away their grisly cargo. She didn't go out to meet the crowd that had gathered on the street. After a moment she turned and took the curving staircase to Dora Hope's bedroom on the second floor.

As the deputy returned to his post at the courtroom doors, Judge Blair gave Scout a questioning look that drew no answer from the prosecutor's carefully controlled features. Crandall, back in his place at the defense table, peered at him suspiciously for a moment, then sat back, confident that nothing had happened that would affect his defense. Gannon continued writing as if nothing existed for him beyond the trial.

"McCall," greeted the prosecutor, approaching the defendant. "Mister" caught in his throat. "This is not the first time you have claimed that Wild Bill Hickok killed your brother, is it? Nor is it the first time you have failed to produce witnesses to support that assertion."

"Is that a question?" It was a snarl. McCall was gripping his knees again, looking like a poorly wrought statue of an Egyptian pharaoh.

"Why is it that no one has come forward to back you up?"

"My crowd moves around a lot. I reckon they're hard to locate."

"Non-existent people always are." Out of the corner of his eye he glimpsed Crandall start to rise and said, "I'm sorry, Your Honor. I withdraw the comment." When the judge nodded: "You said that Hickok 'went for one of his pistols' when he saw you approaching from behind in the saloon on August second. Did you mean one of the derringers in his side pockets? One of the Colts in his sash? Perhaps even his shotgun lying nearby?"

"I don't know which he was after. He moved and I let him have it."

"Why is it that you alone witnessed this maneuver?"

"Maybe it's because I wasn't Wild Bill's friend, like them others," he sneered. "Maybe they seen what they wanted to."

"Why didn't you go around in front of Wild Bill and shoot him in the face like a man?"

"I didn't want to commit suicide."

The spectators broke into raucous laughter. Blair banged for order. Scout half-smiled and waited patiently for the mirth to subside, knowing that the exchange would be repeated far and wide and become part of the legend. It was a strange moment. He had the feeling that every move he made was part of some prearranged pattern he couldn't break out of if he tried. What sort of man had Hickok been that he could exercise such influence over the lives of others months after his own was finished?

"Do you still maintain that revenge was your only motive in wanting to kill Hickok?" The question lashed out in the gulf of silence that followed the gallery's merriment.

"I do. He killed my brother Andy, like I said, with a hoe."

Scout shook his head. He had one hand in his trousers pocket and was leaning on the other atop the rail before the witness box. "That won't do."

McCall's one normal eye focused on him, and for the first time since the trial had begun he smiled. His remaining teeth were the color of tobacco and speckled black. "Prove otherwise."

"I intend to." The prosecutor turned his back on him. "What do you do for a living?"

He didn't see the defendant shrug, but he knew he had. "Odd jobs, mostly. Some prospecting. Whatever I can get."

"Is it lucrative?" Getting no answer, he rephrased it. "Do you make much money?"

McCall snorted. "Hell, no. I'm damned lucky if I eat."

"Where did you get the money to play poker with Hickok on August first?"

There was a pause, then, "I don't rightly remember."

"You don't?" Scout turned around. "You just said you were lucky when you made enough to eat, yet you don't remember where you obtained enough to sit in on a game with a professional gambler. It seems to me that would be a high-water mark in any drifter's life."

"Well, I don't."

"Perhaps I can refresh your memory." The prosecutor rested his forearms on the rail, bringing his face level with McCall's and within six inches of it. His voice sank, accordingly, to a conversational tone that was nonetheless audible all over the still room. "Did John Varnes and Tim Brady pay you to dispose of James Butler Hickok in the interests of keeping Deadwood a wide-open town?"

"Objection!" Crandall's bellow sounded twice as loud after Scout's insinuating murmur. "The prosecution has introduced no evidence to support this hypothesis."

Scout ignored him, his eyes still on McCall. "Isn't John Varnes the man you told the authorities placed a bounty on Hickok's head, and wasn't Tim Brady his partner?"

"Objection! Objection! Your Honor!"

"You're going to the gallows, McCall. Why should you drop through the trap alone?"

"Your Honor!" Crandall demanded.

Blair employed his gavel angrily. "That will be enough, counselor. If you have nothing solid upon which to base this line of inquiry, I'll be forced to throw it out."

"He has nothing, Your Honor," said the General, triumph gleaming in his eyes. "My esteemed opponent is running a tremendous bluff."

Scout was reluctant to remove his gaze from McCall's, which had ceased to be hostile and had drawn inward. He knew what was going through the killer's mind. There had been no mention of Tim Brady in his short-lived statement made in the Yankton jail.

"You heard me, counselor," the judge said acidly. "The statement you mentioned is not a legal document because the defendant did not sign it, and thus it cannot be used in evidence. You will have to offer something more concrete."

"I can do that, Your Honor." The prosecutor straightened and faced the bench. "John Varnes is in federal custody at this moment. His partner, Tim Brady, is dead, killed by federal officers while resisting arrest."

Blair was so taken aback that he nearly neglected to gavel down the excited buzz that had started in the gallery. Crandall stared accusingly at his client as if this were his fault.

"Varnes has been charged with conspiracy to commit murder?" asked the judge.

"No formal charges have been preferred as yet, Your Honor. He was apprehended less than an hour ago."

"Then he can have made no statement as yet." The judge considered. "Will both counsels please approach the bench?" When Scout and Crandall had complied, Blair leaned toward the prosecutor. "I trust Mrs. Sargent is all right?"

"I'm told that all the hostages are safe, Your Honor." Scout's relief and joy were evident in spite of his attempt to appear emotionless. He wished he were with Grace right then.

"I am pleased for you both."

"Thank you, Your Honor."

Crandall winked. Scout supposed that was as close as he came to congratulating anyone.

"Mr. Scout," said Blair, "in the light of this new development, would you like to recess until a statement has been obtained from the arrested party?"

Scout hesitated only an instant. "With respect, Your Honor, if I thought I had not the evidence to convict the defendant going into these proceedings I would not have brought this case before you."

The judge raised his eyebrows. "Then you wish to proceed?"

"I do, Your Honor." He derived secret satisfaction from the expression on the General's face, a mixture of astonishment and distrust.

"You understand that I will have to sustain General Crandall's objection to your present line and forbid you to continue with it?" asked the judge.

"I do, Your Honor," Scout repeated. It made him feel oddly like a bridegroom. He thought of Grace.

Blair seemed on the verge of asking another question, then shook his head. "Very well. With your permission I'll rule."

"You knew going into it what would happen, didn't you?" Bartholomew asked when Scout was beside him again and the judge was instructing the jury to ignore the prosecution's references to

Varnes, Brady and the statement attributed to the accused regarding the former.

Scout didn't answer his partner's question. "Did you box in college, Tessie?"

"I was too busy reading up on precedents. Why?"

"First you feint, then you jab."

Jack McCall had been on the stand so long that he was beginning to look at home. Not wanting to destroy his complacency just yet, the prosecutor remained behind the table when he asked his next question.

"Returning to the afternoon of August second," he said. "You're certain Hickok observed your approach from behind?"

"He had to. Like I said, he went for a pistol. I figure he seen me reflected in his shot glass. I said that too."

"Could he have heard you?"

The defendant laughed, a short, harsh bark. "It won't do you no good to try and trip me up. He couldn't of heard me, on account of he was arguing with Cap'n Massey at the time, like I said. Besides, he had to of recognized me in the glass or he wouldn't of went for no weapon. He knowed I was angry at him for making sport of me after I got beat the day before. He seen me, all right."

"Curved glass distorts reflections, McCall." Scout was coming around the end of the table, pressing hard. "No man with ordinary vision could recognize another's features in anything so inadequate as an ounce whiskey glass."

"That's where I got you, Mr. Prosecutor." McCall clenched and unclenched his hands on his knees in malicious glee. "Wild Bill's eyesight was more than just ordinary. He could pick the ass off an ant at forty paces. Ask anyone who seen him shoot. A steady hand ain't worth a good goddamn without a good eye to go with it."

"No, Mr. Defendant," mocked Scout quietly, stopping halfway between the table and the witness. "That's where I've got you. Were you aware that at the time of his death, James Butler Hickok was going blind?"

The word "blind" hummed through the courtroom like electric current. McCall looked confused.

"That's a lie!" he shouted.

"Is it?" Scout donned his glasses. "I have a letter from the proprietor of a variety theater in Cheyenne, Wyoming Territory"—with the timing of practiced teamwork he thrust a hand behind him just in time to collect the manila folder from Bartholomew—"in which he states that on March second of this year, Hickok told him: 'My eyes are getting bad. The best that I can do with them now is to see a man's form, indistinctly, at sixteen paces. My shooting days are over.'" He held up the letter for all to see as he revolved on his heel, stopping finally before the bench, whereupon he handed it to the judge. Blair put on his own spectacles.

"Can you produce this witness, counselor?" he asked, once he had read the epistle.

"I couldn't locate him, Your Honor. He has moved since writing me and left no forwarding address."

"Ha!" snorted Crandall.

Blair peered at the defender over the top of his glasses. "Is that some new form of objection, General?"

Crandall rose, shaking his head. "If Your Honor pleases, I will rely upon the old-fashioned kind. That letter could have been written by anyone, and even if its author is whom Mr. Scout says he is, we have not the pleasure of his company in this court where his testimony would be under oath. Even then it would be hearsay and thus inadmissible."

"The bench will decide what is inadmissible, counselor. You know very well that statements made by the deceased in a murder case carry greater weight than those of a third party. But the rest of your objection is well taken. If the prosecution cannot produce the author of this letter, or, failing that, a deposition signed and sworn to in the presence of a reliable witness, I will have to dismiss this as evidence."

"The prosecution can do better than that, Your Honor." Relishing the moment, Scout opened the folder again and drew out a sheaf of closely typewritten pages. "This is a deposition signed by Dr. E. A. Thurston, the ranking medical authority at Camp Carlin, Wyoming Territory, whom Hickok consulted shortly before his marriage to Agnes Thatcher Lake on March fifth, sworn to before a notary and bearing his seal. With the court's permission I would like it tagged as evidence."

Blair riffled through the pages, stopping to read a passage here and there, then nodded and handed it to the diminutive clerk, who marked a corner of the top sheet with his pen and returned it. The judge passed it back down to Scout.

"'The patient, J. B. Hickok, complained of severe pain and blurring of vision in the left eye,'" he read. "'Examination of the eyeball revealed abnormal pressure impeding the natural drainage of internal fluid and depressing the optic disc in the pattern referred to in medical parlance as "cupping." These are the classic symptoms of advanced glaucoma. Tests conducted upon the patient's right eye disclosed similar conditions to a less advanced degree. Both were inoperable, and it is the expert opinion of this physician that the patient would soon be completely blind.'" The prosecutor looked up, his eyes shearing daggerlike through dead silence to the defendant's. His voice dropped dramatically. "Jack McCall, do you still say that the man you killed recognized your reflection in a glass scarcely larger than a thimble and forced you to shoot him in your own defense?"

Crandall stood in an attempt to break the spell. It didn't bend. "Nicely done, counselor. I applaud your sense of theater. But where is your corroboration?"

Scout's gaze remained locked with McCall's. "That was a second opinion, which I read first because of its use of language comprehensible to the layman. I have another, dryer and more technical, signed and sworn to by the doctor who attempted and failed to alleviate Hickok's ailment earlier at the army hospital in Rochester, New York. He was suffering acutely from his condition at the time, which may account for his bad temper while traveling with William Cody's theatrical troupe. Certainly it would explain his violent reaction upon his first exposure to bright spotlights. That doctor also diagnosed his problem as glaucoma and declared it inoperable. I would now like to introduce his deposition into evidence."

In the excitement following the presentation of the second affidavit, few heard the stunned defense counsel rest the case for Jack McCall.

"Eleven cents, sir."

Scout flipped the driver a coin and trotted up the walk to the Sargent mansion without waiting for change. It was still daylight out, and bitter cold. Just as he reached the veranda a gray-haired man came out carrying a black bag and touched his hat on his way past.

The prosecutor was about to ask him something when Grace came to the door. They were in each other's arms in an instant. The black maid, who had been on her way to the door, spun about sharply and vanished through the arch opposite. The front door swung shut of its own weight, or perhaps Grace helped it with a push.

"Are you all right?" Scout asked anxiously, when they came up for air. "That was a doctor's bag I saw."

There was a dreamlike glaze over her dusty-blue eyes. "He was here to see Mother. Don't worry, Marshal Burdick got us all out without a scratch."

"Remind me to send him a case of imported cigars." He felt suddenly guilty for his relief. "How is your mother?"

"She's well." She showed no inclination to disengage herself from his arms. If anything, the way she was leaning forced him to keep them around her to prevent her from falling. He didn't feel put upon. "That's all I can say, she's well. I had thought that the shock of the experience might help her overcome the state she's been in since Edgar's death. She cried when we were rescued. That's what's been missing these past two years, her crying. But the doctor wasn't so sure. He said we'll have to wait and see. Doctors are always telling people to wait." Her voice was empty.

He held her tighter. He felt a sudden, frightening urge to crush her, he wanted to possess her that much. He restrained himself, but the effort involved frightened him even more. He had never known that love was mixed so heavily with fear.

"I was insanely afraid for you," he heard himself saying, his words muffled by her hair. It smelled of herbs and something else that made his heart pound. "If I'd had a gun I would have killed McCall for being responsible for what had happened. But I did the next best thing; I hanged him with his own words."

"Is the trial over?"

"We're in dinner recess for an hour before final summations. Bartholomew had to hold me down to keep me from bolting while Blair was going for his gavel. I was the first one out the door when court adjourned."

"I stayed here to find out what the doctor had to say." She was quivering. "It was terrible, waiting to see you. The room kept shrinking and I paced holes through my shoes. I was hurrying to get my wrap when you came. Oh, Julian, what if we had passed each other on the way?"

"We didn't." Filtered through his chest, his voice was an almost imperceptible rumble, infinitely reassuring. She held him so hard her arms ached.

For a long time neither of them spoke, locked together in the drafty entranceway, swaying unconsciously. Grace, her face pressed to Julian's vest, could hardly breathe but took no notice of the discomfort. He smelled of tobacco and broadcloth and man. She forgot about Edgar and the house, about the man who had died in the kitchen and the one who had died out back, about the marshal and the trial, and if she didn't entirely forget about her mother, she at least placed her in an insulated corner of her mind for the present. There was simply no more room in the rest of it for anyone but Julian.

BOOK THREE

THE VERDICT

I never killed one man without good cause.

—James Butler Hickok, 1867

CHAPTER 20

Julian Scout looked at the jury for some time before he spoke, scrutinizing in turn each of the faces he had been watching for three days and wondering if he would recognize any of their owners if they met on the street tomorrow. Their life histories were lost in the jumble of his thoughts, leaving him with nothing but their names. It occurred to him that McCall probably didn't even know those, and he thought it strange that a man should be so unfamiliar with the men who were to decide his fate. But when he commenced his address there was no pity in his tone for the man in the dock.

"'Reasonable doubt' is a phrase with an elusive meaning," he began quietly. A pacer, he quartered the floor before the jury box slowly, back and forth, back and forth, hands clasped behind his back, mesmerizing the jurors with the metronomic movement and the rise and fall of his voice. "It means that unless the prosecution has failed to demonstrate the probability of the defendant's guilt, it is the duty of the jury to deliver a verdict of guilty.

"In the case of the People of the United States versus Jack McCall, the prosecution has gone far beyond that. We have shown that in spite of the defense's attempts to impugn his character, James Butler Hickok was a law-abiding citizen engaged in a legal and harmless activity at the time of his treacherous death. We have examined his record as a public servant and found it exemplary. Two of our country's greatest heroes have come forward, one posthumously, to testify to his sterling qualities. The example of his brief and stormy career in the show business should be enough to establish his modesty and unwillingness to parade his greatness before an adoring multitude. We have shown him to be honest and brave beyond the ability of most men, generous and a true friend to those in need. Can we forget so easily the many favors he did for William Cody at a time when the latter, a nearly destitute youth unable to repay him with anything other than friendship, required them most?

"What has the defense offered in rebuttal? The dubious testimony of a self-confessed assassin who was neither in Deadwood's Saloon No. 10 at the time Hickok was killed, nor in Abilene at the time his partner gambled with his life and lost—which is what he was called upon to tell us about. The lies of a man in the shadow of the noose willing to say anything to escape his fate. Hearsay. Semantics."

Scout stopped pacing and turned to face the jury, his hands braced against the rail in front of the box. His eyes burned slowly as he took in their faces once again, one by one.

"We have shown," he continued, "a lawman at the end of his life, unable because of his failing eyesight to trust his skill with revolvers, the Prince of Pistoleers reduced to carrying a shotgun for his own protection. We have shown a common saloon swamper, a moral and financial failure who, consumed with hatred and envy, with malice aforethought and in full view of witnesses, slunk up behind the closest thing to established law and order the city of Deadwood had ever known and slew him in cold blood without ever giving him a chance to defend himself."

His tone grew intense. "What do they say about us in the East, where men meet to judge our actions and plot our future? 'Barbarians!' they cry. 'Animals, who would look on as Cain slew Abel and applaud the deed.' And they are right!

"How many times have the McCalls of this world escaped justice in frontier courts? How many widows and children curse our names because we have failed to avenge the lives of their husbands and fathers? Hickok left a widow. Is there one here who will dry her bitter tears should the murderer of her champion cheat his destiny a second time?"

Roaring now, he thrust an avenging finger at McCall, who sat glaring back at him from behind the defense table. "Every moment this man lives, every foul breath he draws, brings the mark of Cain down heavier upon our brows. The time is long past due when the decent men of this territory must rise and cast away the evil that dwells among them as the Lord in His wisdom consigned Satan to the fires of Hell. I only pray that it is not already too late."

Again he paused, his gaze blazing across the double row of faces before him like flames of retribution. When he resumed speaking it was in a whisper, as if the effort of defending Hickok's good name had claimed his last ounce of strength. "Gentlemen of the jury, if there is any justice in your hearts, you must find the defendant, Jack McCall, guilty of murder in the first degree."

He had no idea how long he stood there after he finished speaking, but silence still lay heavy in the room as he turned and retraced his steps to the prosecution table. The spell remained unbroken as General John Quincy Adams Crandall rose and hooked his fat thumbs inside his vest pockets. He didn't approach the jury.

"I ask you, gentlemen," he said slowly, "to picture a twelve-year-old boy returning home from an adolescent fishing expedition with his dying little brother cradled in his arms, the blood from his broken head leaking over the older boy's hands and staining his clothes. Now I ask you to picture that same boy growing up in the shadow of his brother's life unavenged, forced to read and hear accounts of the unpunished felon's escapades described in terms of unabashed veneration. Finally, I ask you to picture that boy, a man now, arriving in Deadwood to find his brother's murderer established in a position of respectability, going about his business as he has time and again since his long-forgotten crime. Forgotten, that is, by all but one.

"A financial failure? Undoubtedly true, but what measure of a man is his station? Jesus was a carpenter. A moral failure? That has not been established, but who are we to judge the effect upon a man of a horror witnessed in his childhood?

"But let us return to Deadwood, and place ourselves once again in the position of this man who is no longer a boy. What would you do?" His eyes sought those of a ruddy-complexioned juror in the second row, who was built like a teamster. "Disgrace your brother's memory by allowing this profane abomination to continue? Mortgage your conscience for fear of retribution?

"Or would you take action?" His hands slapped the table top in thunderous punctuation, startling the room's occupants with its violence. "Would you breathe a prayer in your brother's memory, seize a weapon, and remove the object of your hatred and shame from the face of the earth as you would lance a festering boil? I ask you to answer that question with your hearts and decide whether Jack McCall is innocent of the charge of first-degree murder on the grounds of justifiable homicide."

It was a brief summation, and everyone, including Judge Blair, was surprised by its abrupt conclusion. But Blair recovered quickly and asked Scout if he wished to rebut. The prosecutor declined.

"There being no objections," the judge continued, "I shall now present the jury with its charges."

CHAPTER 21

Scout was having trouble getting a fire going in the grate. He stabbed viciously at the stubborn embers with the poker, receiving only a smudged coat sleeve for his efforts. At length he gave up with a curse, dropped the instrument clanging to the flagged hearth, and threw himself heavily into the leather armchair. Bartholomew, who had been filling his snuff box from a humidor atop his desk, set it down and lent his talents to the task. In five minutes the logs were enveloped in rosy yellow flame.

"You shouldn't let it get to you, Julian," he said, warming his backside. "Sometimes I think you put too much of yourself into a case."

The prosecutor glared at him. "When did you ever know me not to?"

"It's a complicated case. You've got to expect the jury to take its time deliberating."

"Three hours ought to be enough to decide anything. They retired at seven. It's now ten after ten. I'll bet they're playing cards."

"We've done everything we can do. It's out of our hands."

"That's what bothers me." He glowered at the fire. "I don't know about this democracy of ours, Tessie. We don't appoint a judge unless we're absolutely certain that his education and experience are suitable for the job. A lawyer can't plead a case until he's passed a rigorous bar examination. Expert witnesses have to be proven as such before their testimony is admitted. Then we turn around and hand the most important decision in the case to a dozen amateurs. Why the hell do we do that, Tessie?"

"You should know the answer to that better than anyone. You've faced professional juries."

Scout thought back to his army days, and the grim tribunal in dress uniforms before whom he had pleaded the case for the 12th

New Hampshire. "I'd forgotten," he said, and fell silent. After a while he looked at his partner. "Did we do everything we could have, Tessie? I can't tell anymore."

"Short of manufacturing evidence and pressuring our witnesses into committing perjury, we covered every square inch of ground open to us. Would you have done more?" There was reproach in his tone.

"You know that's not what I meant. I have these same doubts at the end of every case. It's like going away on vacation and not being able to enjoy yourself because you can't remember if you locked the front door." He scooped his abandoned pipe out of the ashtray on the arm of the chair. It was cold.

"All right, suppose we've lost. So what? It's not the end of the world; certainly it's not the end of yours."

"What do you mean?" Having his worst fear expressed shocked the prosecutor.

Bartholomew made an impatient noise. "Lincoln dropped more than one important case," he explained, exasperated. "Who remembers? The point is you're famous. Everyone who reads newspapers knows your name. They're the ones who mark ballots, not dead, half-blind gunmen or their widows."

Scout stared at him. For the first time he failed to see his friend staring back. The face he saw—eager, half-illumined by the flames— left him with an empty feeling in the pit of his stomach. "My God," he said in his awe. "Do you really think that's what I care about? Climbing into office up a hangman's rope?"

"Don't act like you're horrified." Bartholomew's expression reminded him of General Crandall's sharklike smile. "Every worthwhile job that exists has been obtained over someone's dead body, either literally or figuratively. You're too good an attorney to go on scraping up someone else's leavings. I told you at the beginning this case can make you."

"And I said I like it fine right where I am. If you want to use this case to put someone in office, run for it yourself. I don't want any part of it."

"You're tired. Why don't you go see Grace?" The senior lawyer's tone was smoothly solicitous. Scout found it suggestive, even lewd.

"I did," he snapped. "She said I was too keyed up and to come see her after the verdict is announced."

"You'd better marry her. She's smarter than both of us."

"I intend to."

Maliciously, Scout savored his partner's astonishment. Bartholomew had been speaking sarcastically; the prosecutor had not. "I guess I forgot to tell you," he said, casually lighting his pipe. "I proposed this afternoon. She accepted."

The other had opened his mouth to protest when someone knocked at the door. It was the bailiff.

"Sir, the jury is back."

At the door Scout paused. "I don't want you to think it wasn't a good partnership, Tessie."

"Gentlemen of the jury, have you reached a verdict?"

Blair's question had a singsong quality, as of a phrase so often repeated that it no longer held any meaning.

"We have, Your Honor."

The foreman, John Treadway, was a slight, clerkish-looking man who displayed none of the outward signs of authority usually to be found in one elected by his fellow jurors to speak for the body. He wore tinted spectacles and held a scrap of paper in his folded hands.

"The defendant will rise."

McCall came up slowly, his chains rattling. His expression was stony. Crandall and Gannon rose too, flanking him. The gaunt attorney had been writing up to that moment, convincing his partner that his copious notes had nothing to do with the affair at hand.

The bailiff collected the paper from the foreman and walked it over to the judge, who unfolded it, adjusted his spectacles to peer at the contents, and handed it back with a nod. It was returned to Treadway.

"We the jury find the defendant guilty as charged."

For the second time since the trial had opened there was a general sigh in the courtroom, as of Destiny placing the final period at the end of the legend. It swelled to a roar. The last of the newspapermen made a beeline for the hallway. Scout closed his eyes for an instant, exhausted suddenly, then swung his attention to McCall. The defendant had paled but his expression hadn't changed. The prosecutor thought: *This is how he must have looked as he was squeezing the trigger*. Crandall's face was angry red, but he didn't appear surprised. Gannon looked bored.

"Your Honor," announced Crandall, raising his voice above the disturbance, "the defense wishes to go on record in opposition to this verdict."

"Such will be noted." This time Blair waited until conditions were right to quell the noise with his gavel. When he had attained a modicum of peace:

"The defendant is hereby returned to the custody of the United States Marshal to await sentencing in this court on January third."

Bartholomew whispered, "No suspense there. There's only one sentence for murder in the first degree."

Scout wasn't listening. As the judge was speaking, he had glimpsed movement out of the corner of his eye and turned to see a tall, well-built man carrying a worn coat and hat making his way to the aisle. As he stepped into the clear, Lorenzo Hickok looked at the prosecutor, nodded, and strode away in the direction of the double doors. His shoulders were squared. The prosecutor wondered if they would remain that way once he had passed beyond sight.

"This court is adjourned," rapped Judge Blair.

CHAPTER 22

"Dear Mr. McCall," the letter began.

The Yankton *Daily Press and Dakotaian* would be pleased and honored to publish posthumously your true account of the slaying of Wild Bill, which you have so generously offered to write. As I am sure you are aware, this journal championed your cause throughout the period of your trial and appeal, and does not intend to surrender the fight until your good name is cleared. A representative will be present upon the execution grounds tomorrow morning to accept your manuscript.

It was signed by the editor of the newspaper.

The prisoner read the letter for the hundredth time, then crumpled it into a ball and tossed it into the far darkened corner of the cell. He squinted at his immature scrawl on the page resting on his knee and shifted his position on the edge of the cot to catch more of the failing light. Inmates had been denied lamps since one of them had burned to death in a desperate attempt to force the guards to open his door. McCall wondered if this was the cell in which the tragedy had occurred. That would account for the stench.

He cursed at yet another clumsy phrase and tried to scratch it out with his worn stump of pencil, tearing the paper in the process and marking the dingily striped knee of his prison trousers. Writing wasn't as easy as it looked. At length, when it was almost pitch dark, he finished and sank back against the clammy stone wall to rest.

He thought of his brother Andy, and of the years since they had last seen each other, but it was all a jumble of saloons and brothels and temporary towns built of canvas and clapboard on muddy streets, blurred behind an alcoholic haze. He couldn't pick out a single face except Hickok's, and he couldn't be sure if he remembered it personally or from one of the hundreds of red-gold rotogravures that had sprung up in the windows of photographers' studios across the territory since Wild Bill's death. Thinking about it made his head ache worse. It ached all the time now since he had been denied whiskey, but at least the shakes and chills of his first days without it were over.

He must have slept, because for a long time he couldn't remember thinking about anything, but when he opened his eyes the cell was still dark. A steam whistle blatted in the distance and was silent. After a while a growling of men's voices reached him unintelligibly, carried across the surface of the James. There were other sounds from time to time, impossible to identify, lost as they were in the great hollow of night.

Again he slept, or seemed to. He was in a saloon playing poker with men he knew, but he didn't know what the game was and when he looked at his cards they were blank. He asked the dealer for three, but they, too, were blank. Then he saw movement reflected in a shot glass before him and recognized his own face beyond his right shoulder, above the muzzle of a revolver. He saw a tongue of flame and then an invisible fist struck him in the back of the head. He awoke screaming.

But no guard appeared, and he decided that he had dreamed the scream as well as the shot. He was sweating and his clothes felt clammy against his skin. It was still dark. From down the corridor came a dry, racking cough. That would be Shidroe, the man who came on at ten. He wondered how long he had been on duty.

He picked up the nightmare from the first blank hand of cards and willed it to change. This time he was in the position of the man with the revolver. He rolled back the hammer and was squeezing the trigger when the seated man turned his head and he recognized his brother's profile, grown up. His finger moved spasmodically and the profile dissolved behind a red smear. Andy fell out of the chair sideways, to reveal Hickok rising across from him with one of his Navy Colts in hand. McCall screamed and fired again, but nothing happened and when he glanced down he saw that his revolver had changed into a pencil stub. Hickok's Colt roared.

He started awake with the taste of brass in his mouth. It was still dark. "God," he said aloud, "I hope I never have another night like this." Then he remembered.

The next time he dreamed he was back in the courtroom, which was a welcome change. Everyone was who he was supposed to be, even the jury foreman, who was standing in the box. Again he heard the guilty verdict. Again he felt nothing; the despair would come later, after the shock wore off. But this time, instead of adjourning, the judge climbed down from the bench and, his robes rustling, stepped to the side door and pulled it open. Hickok strode in carrying both revolvers.

Spotting McCall at the defense table, he turned half toward him and raised the Colt in his right hand to shoulder level, sighting down his outstretched arm. McCall tried to duck beneath the table but was stopped by an iron grip on each shoulder. He glanced right and left and was horrified to see that he was being held by General Crandall and Julian Scout. Desperately he sought an ally, but the only other person within reach was Orville Gannon, busy scribbling notes and paying no attention to what was going on around him. Hickok fired. McCall awoke choking on his own tongue. There was still no light in the cell.

Like a nickel slug the nightmare kept returning. Sometimes he was the man doing the shooting, other times he was on the receiving end. In all of them he ended up getting killed. Then he would wake up and find his surroundings dark as ever. He wondered if he'd been hanged already and this was hell.

When finally he jolted out of his last hallucination and found that the gray illumination of dawn had begun to bleed into the stygian night, he got down on his hands and knees and groped about the floor until he found the sheet upon which he had written his account of Hickok's killing. Slowly he tore it into bits so tiny no one would ever be able to put them back together.

From the Yankton *Daily Press and Dakotaian,* March 1, 1877 (evening edition):

At half-past nine, everything being in readiness, the condemned man bade farewell to his fellow prisoners, and left his prison house for the last time. There were present at the time L. D. F. Poore, representing the New York *Herald;* Bryant, reporter for a New England journal; Dr. Wixson and the Taylor Bros. of the Dakota *Herald;* and Phil K. Faulk, representing the *Press and Dakotaian.* . . .

Upon leaving the jail, Marshal Burdick, with Deputy Marshal Ash, occupied a light carriage and led the way. They were followed by a carriage containing McCall, with Rev. Father Daxacher and his assistant J. A. Curry, Deputy Marshal C. P. Edmunds, and ourself. The mournful train, bearing its living victim to the grave, was preceded and followed by a long line of vehicles of every description, with hundreds on horseback and on foot, all leading north, out through Broadway. Not a word was spoken during the ride of two miles to the school section north of the Catholic cemetery. McCall still continuing to bear up bravely, even after the gallows loomed in full view. At ten o'clock precisely the place of execution was reached.

As soon as possible after reaching the place, the prisoner mounted the platform of the gallows, accompanied by Deputy Marshal Ash. Here he evinced the same firmness and nerve that have always characterized him since his arrest and trial. He placed himself in the center of the platform facing east and gazed out over the throng without exhibiting the least faltering; not even a quiver of the lip. U. S. Marshal Burdick, with Deputy Ash, Rev. Father Daxacher, and his assistant, Mr. Curry, were the only parties upon the platform.

Immediately the limbs of the unfortunate culprit were pinioned, when he knelt with his spiritual counsel. Turning his face toward Heaven his lips were seen to move in prayer. Upon rising he kissed the crucifix and after the black cap had been placed over his face, the U.S. marshal placed the noose around his neck. He then said: "Wait one moment, Marshal, until I pray."

Marshal Burdick waited until he had uttered a prayer and then adjusted the noose, when he said, "Draw it tighter, Marshal." All was now in readiness, and the assemblage of nearly one thousand persons seemed to hold their breath. At precisely fifteen minutes after ten o'clock the trap was sprung, and with the single choking expression, "Oh, God," uttered while the drop fell, the body of Jack McCall was dangling between Heaven and Earth. The drop was four feet, and everything having been carefully arranged there was but a brief struggle with the King of Terrors.

With a shudder, Grace Scout finished reading the front page account and laid the newspaper atop a convenient packing crate. The entrance hall was stacked high with them, stuffed full of books and dishes and clothing and items of sentimental value, all awaiting the movers who would transport them across town to the Scouts' new home down the street from the courthouse. The newlywed wife was pulling on her gloves when Dora Hope came in, adjusting her wrap.

"Are you ready, dear?"

"As soon as Julian gets back with our new carriage," replied Grace. "Have you read about the hanging? The paper's over there." She glanced in the mirror next to the door, checking to see if her freckles were effectively concealed by powder.

"Leave it for the movers," said her mother. "Life is short enough without wasting time reading about other people's deaths."

A carriage rattled up outside.

> Merchants Hotel,
> Louisville, Kentucky,
> February 25, 1877.

To the Marshal of Yankton:

Dear Sir:

I saw in the morning papers a piece about the sentence of the murderer of Wild Bill, Jack McCall. There was a young man of the name John McCall left here about six years ago, who has not been heard from for the last three years. He has a father, mother, and three sisters living here in Louisville, who are very uneasy about him since they heard about the murder of Wild Bill. If you can send us any information about him, we would be very thankful to you.

This John McCall is about twenty-five years old, has light hair, inclined to curl, and one eye crossed. I cannot say about his height, as he was not grown when he left here. Please write as soon as convenient, as we are very anxious to hear from you.

> Very respectfully,
> Mary A. McCall.

Marshal Burdick, who had found the letter on his desk upon his return from the Catholic cemetery, where he had been busy chasing souvenir hunters from Jack McCall's day-old grave, started to crumple the letter preparatory to hurling it into his wastebasket, then thought better of it, smoothed it out, and placed it in his top drawer. It was part of the legend.

EPILOGUE

DEAD MAN'S RAFFLE

The Black Hills shimmer in the summer heat, nervous fingers twitching and stirring with Deadwood cupped in them like a bad hand of poker. They are not black at all except from a distance, but blue and green and purple, and from the streams that flow down their slopes lived the Cheyenne and then the Sioux, who venerated the low, rolling mountains as a sacred place where spirits dwelled. Now white men pan gold from those streams and strip the color from the hills to reveal the naked black soil beneath, justifying the name they gave them.

On a hillside overlooking the town, a mound of fresh earth lies at the foot of a broad tree stump, in the bark of which is cut a crude legend:

> A brave man, the victim of an
> assassin, J. B. Hickok (Wild
> Bill) age 48 years; murdered by
> Jack McCall, Aug. 2, 1876

In death as in life, Hickok's existence is shrouded in uncertainty, for the anonymous carver has incorrectly advanced his age nine years. There are fresh flowers on the grave, which some attribute to Calamity Jane Canary, a female hell raiser whose reputation has taken a sharp upward swing since the pistoleer's death. Some say they were secretly married. Others maintain that it was a secret even to Hickok. But the legend that Calamity Jane chased the fleeing McCall around a butcher's shop with a cleaver following Wild

Bill's murder will continue long after her death in a new century. By her own request, she will be buried within twenty feet of Hickok's grave.

This is not, however, his final resting place. On August 3, 1879, old friends J. S. McClintock, Charlie Utter, and Lewis Schoenfield will disinter the remains for burial in Mount Moriah Cemetery. They will find that the combination of minerals in the earth has resulted in a natural embalming, and that three years after his demise Hickok's body will hold true to Doc Pierce's description while preparing it for interment in 1876: "I have seen many dead men on the field of battle and in civil life, but Wild Bill was the prettiest corpse I have ever seen." But for some shrinkage of the flesh, he will look as he did the day he played his last hand, with fingers like marble clutching the Sharps rifle with which he was buried. The righteous will say that the earth rejected him because of his wicked deeds.

With the move, a more impressive slab will be erected over the new site, reading:

WILD BILL
J. B. HICKOK
Killed by the Assassin
Jack McCall
Deadwood City
Black Hills
August 2, 1876
Pard, we will meet again in the happy
hunting grounds to part no more.
Good Bye
Colorado Charlie

Souvenir hunters will chip at the stone until nothing remains of the legend. In 1892 it will be replaced by a monument that will be destroyed, in turn, after which a steel fence will encircle the plot and a new stone.

Today there is no one at the grave. Most of Deadwood has gathered in front of the tent Hickok shared with Charlie Utter, where Wild Bill's effects are being raffled off at twenty-five cents a chance to defray the expense of the funeral. Aside from a trail of fable that will swell and spread like the smoke from a passing locomotive, he

has left little behind: A brown leather valise with the initials
J. B. H. carved on the rolled handle; two broad-brimmed hats, one
for working, one for show; one suit of fine quality, the jacket spe-
cially designed to swing open freely for swift access to a revolver;
several blinding white linen shirts, intricately pleated; a beaded and
fringed buckskin shirt; dusty work clothes; a black oilcloth slicker; a
linen duster; red flannel underwear; two pairs of dress boots, one pair
polished to a high black finish, the other of immaculate brushed
buckskin; a red silk sash; a pair of leather work boots, scuffed and
worn down at the heels; some ties; a gold watch; assorted prospecting
equipment; guns. His pack animals belong to Utter and his corpse is
wearing everything else.

Among the firearms are a sawed-off shotgun, three Navy Colts,
two with ivory handles, a Deane-Adams English five-shot revolver,
and matched derringers. There are also boxes of ammunition for all
seven weapons, as well as for the Sharps in the coffin, and a bowie
knife, well used.

The clothing goes first, and for the next few weeks the citizens of
Deadwood will be treated to the spectacle of hardrock miners and
half-breed Sioux parading around in fine linen and a Prince Albert
designed for a larger frame. Budding entrepreneurs, blessed with
greater foresight, will cut up the boots and buckskin shirt to make
tobacco pouches and sell them for two dollars apiece on the strength
of their original ownership. The gold watch will end up in the possession of an eastern railroad magnate, one of the hats will emerge
many years later in a local miners' museum, and the rest of the
haberdashery will fall by the wayside, destroyed out of ignorance or
indifference, or lost.

The ammunition, a scarce commodity out here where the only
link with civilization is a single stage run to and from Bismarck, will
be used up on Indians, claim jumpers, and faro dealers with an
affinity for the bottom of the deck.

Of the fate of the firearms, little will be known save the following:

The shotgun will kill a bartender in Amarillo, Texas, and be lost
in a fire in a boxcar belonging to a traveling Wild West show.

The plain-handled Colt will vanish without a trace.

The English revolver and one of the ivory-handled Colts will fall
into the hands of private collectors and never be fired again.

The derringers will be lost to posterity, as will the bowie knife. Only the remaining ivory-handled Colt, serial number 139345, with "Wild Bill" engraved on the butt, is destined to play a greater role in history, when Sheriff Pat Garrett uses it to bring an end to the career of New Mexico bandit William "Billy the Kid" Bonney in 1881. Thus will two of the most enduring legends of the old West be forever linked.

POSTSCRIPT

Aces & Eights is not intended to be a factual account of the trial of Jack McCall, although parts of it are based on existing transcripts, and the particulars of Wild Bill Hickok's life have been recorded faithfully. The characters of Julian Scout, T. S. E. Bartholomew, General John Quincy Adams Crandall, and Orville Gannon are fictional interpretations based on the actual attorneys of record on the McCall case. Others, notably Grace Sargent and her mother, Dora Hope, were spun from whole cloth. Federal Judge Blair and U. S. Marshal Burdick existed, presiding, respectively, at the trial and execution of Hickok's killer.

With the exceptions of Buffalo Bill Cody and Ben Thompson, all of the witnesses herein presented gave testimony during the actual proceedings. It is the author's contention that had these famous frontiersmen been available at the time, they would have been summoned.

The most important truth, which remains unaltered, is this: At 3:10 on the afternoon of August 2, 1876, Jack McCall shot and killed James Butler Hickok from behind while the latter was playing poker in Deadwood's Saloon No. 10, and told authorities later that he had done so in return for monies promised him by John Varnes, whose partner was Tim Brady. The author hopes that readers will excuse him for enlarging upon historical fact in pursuit of his theme.